When Good isn't Good Enough

William Tucker always does the right thing. He excels at high school, works at the grocery store, passes out bulletins at his father's church, and still finds time to fight fires as the newest firefighter in Coosa Creek, Alabama.

But no matter how many good deeds William does, it never seems like enough. So when his father's expectations and the community's hypocrisy become too much to bear, William's obsession with doing good transforms into something far more dangerous.

burn

burn

HEATH GIBSON

Woodbury, Minnesota

First Edition
First Printing, 2012

Book design by Bob Gaul
Cover design by Adrienne Zimiga
Cover image © iStockphoto: Stephen Folkes

Flux, an imprint of Llewellyn Worldwide Ltd.

Library of Congress Cataloging-in-Publication Data
Gibson, Heath.
    Burn/Heath Gibson.—1st ed.
        p. cm.
    Summary: High school senior William "Wee Wee" Tucker may not be able to meet his pastor-father's expectations, stop his mother's drinking, or protect his gay brother, but his heroism as a volunteer firefighter has a big impact on his small Alabama town.
    ISBN 978-0-7387-3095-0
    [1. Firefighters—Fiction. 2. Pyromania—Fiction. 3. Family problems—Fiction. 4. Clergy—Fiction. 5. Gays—Fiction. 6. Alcoholism—Fiction.]
    I. Title.
    PZ7.G339293Bur 2012
    [Fic]—dc23
                                                                    2012006179

Flux
Llewellyn Worldwide Ltd.
2143 Wooddale Drive
Woodbury, MN 55125-2989
www.fluxnow.com

Printed in the United States of America

For Michael. Without your friendship,
I would have never even had the idea.

Seemed pretty simple at the time. Fire. Hoses. Water. Heroes. You know, the sirens sound, the flames roar, hell forming right in front of your face. And I could stand right there and beat it back into thin air. Quite a feeling.

What's that? Can't really tell you.

I guess.

Maybe I wanted to be.

When?

DJ.

Then Mandy.

It's kind of like when my daddy preached about baptism, coming out of the waters brand new. He used to say this scripture right before he dunked them: "'I baptize you before he comes, that when he comes, he will baptize you with the Holy Ghost and fire.'"

When you look at it like that, not much of a choice. Like my mom used to say, some things are just as plain as the nose on your face.

I know. That was something that weighed on me at first. But when don't sacrifices have to be made? I figure, whose to say what is and isn't worth it?

Sorry. I get it. You ask the questions.

Yeah, it hurt quite a bit, let me tell you. But sometimes friends hurt each other. Family too.

Fire is my friend.

No, I don't mean it like that. Can't shake hands or hang out. We both just work for the same reason.

I figured you'd be getting to that. Everybody wants to know. But you should know without me telling you.

ONE

Most folks can't understand why somebody would run into burning buildings for a living. So people really don't get why I do it for free—well, almost. Busting into fireballs that used to be double-wide trailers, fighting brush fires that threaten to take a whole year's crops, breathing more smoke than air, ash and soot up your nose and in your mouth. Dragging out old ladies kicking and screaming because you wouldn't let them get their photo albums. And of course, there's that whole possibility of getting burned up and dying. But that's not going to happen, not if you pay attention. Just like Chief Griffin says, "Those caught with their head up their ass might as well kiss it goodbye." Yep, I'm going to get all that for the bargain price of twenty-five dollars a call. So you see, it's got nothing to do with the money.

Heck, my buddy Thad spends more of the money I make at D&G than I do. Can't go two days without Mr. Chunky-Butt bumming a few bucks for chili-cheese burgers or another can of Copenhagen. I keep telling him he doesn't need either one. But I give him the money anyway. Nobody tells Thad no—he's just too fat and funny to turn down.

"Come on now, Wee Wee, don't even act like you're a tight-ass or something. Just two dollars." Thad digs a couple of wadded-up dollar bills and a handful of change out of his pocket and drops them on my tailgate. The change shines under the orange lights in the parking lot of the Winn-Dixie. Yeah, Friday night in Coosa Creek, Alabama, is exciting, let me tell you.

"Thad, why don't you just eat the leftovers?"

"Wee Wee, what in the hell are you talking about?"

I point to his camouflage T-shirt that's got crumbs and cheese stains down the front.

Thad looks down at his shirt, then picks off a piece of jalapeño and pops it in his mouth. He swallows, staring at me like, "So you going to give me the money or not?"

I reach back for my wallet. "Jesus, Thad, when you have a heart attack before we graduate, I don't want to hear nothing about it." I hand him a five.

"Don't let your daddy hear you taking the Lord's name in vain like that." Thad slides off the tailgate. "Remember when he found that beer can in the back of your truck. Made the whole back pew come up in front, preaching how alcohol was the juice of the devil and all that." He turns and walks toward the drive-in on the other side of the parking lot. "I can't handle that kind of guilt, Wee Wee," he says, shoving my money in his pocket.

Thad walks by the pick-up trucks and cars that line up in the parking lot every Friday and Saturday night. He's got to stop and talk to everybody. He calls it making the rounds.

Every weekend is the same. We all just hang out, talking and such, until Deputy Dildo rides by and runs us off at midnight. Every now and then, somebody will do something stupid like show up drunk and fall all over the place, or drag race across the parking lot. That kind of stuff gets us gone quick.

"Hey, Wee Wee." Mandy Pearman calls from the trunk of her Honda Civic.

I smile and wave back because it's impossible to respond to Mandy Pearman and not smile. It doesn't matter that she uses the nickname my sixty-three vertical inches of presence will never let me shake. When somebody who looks like Mandy acknowledges you in public, your brain and your face don't really listen to each other.

"What y'all doing tonight?" Mandy yells. She jumps off her trunk and heads my way.

Unfortunately, I have been subjected to a lifetime of growing up with Mandy, in the same church and class ever since we needed help getting out of the sandbox. Because our families have been friends forever, I've had a front-row seat to the burning-hot specimen she's grown into like a rose bush on steroid fertilizer. It's been a torture no guy's carnal urges should have to endure.

"Oh, you know," I say back.

She steps up in front of me and flips her blond hair back over her shoulder. "You go to the game tonight?" She towers over me. Then again, almost everybody does.

I look down at my red and black D&G Grocery shirt that I have to wear to work.

"Nope."

Now Mandy knows her question didn't make any sense, but she just needed something to say. It would be hard to convince me she's talking to me for any other reason besides being polite. She knows that's what her mom expects.

"Well, it was something else." Mandy's eyes get all wide and she slaps my leg.

My brain takes a second to gather itself after the physical contact. "I'll bet." My throat catches. I quickly clear it. "So, who you here with?" My turn to ask a stupid question.

"Oh, nobody in particular. Just some of the girls who needed a ride from the game."

Mandy Pearman is never with anyone in particular. It's been a mystery of Coosa Creek since eighth grade. She has lots of friends without being in a clique. She dates without having boyfriends. She has simultaneously pulled off popularity and distance. Maybe that's what draws me and just about everybody else.

"Well, you can have a seat here if you want." I know how to be polite too.

Mandy turns around and jumps up on the tailgate next to me. She rests her hand on my shoulder. Don't get your hopes up there. It's not like that. This is just part of the torture. I'm a friend of the family, so light, utterly non-sexual gestures are normal. Guys in middle school were jealous of my special-contact status for about two months before they realized Mandy was more likely to press her lips to an electric fence than to mine. It was a nice two months, though.

"So, you getting ready for homecoming? Just a couple weeks away. I hope you've asked off from work." Mandy swings her legs back and forth with that playful air that makes most people comfortable around her. And for a second I entertain the idea that maybe she's asking me, because I could ask *her*. But it's only a fleeting thought I should know better than to let into my head.

"Haven't given it much thought, come to think of it." Biggest lie I've told to date. "I'll probably have to work, knowing my luck."

"That sucks."

"Tell me about it." But it really doesn't suck. Work bails me out from trying to find a date shorter than me. Guys, it matters. If you don't believe me, watch how many girls slide those heels off before they step in front of the photographer.

"Well, Mama and me are going shopping for a dress tomorrow down in Montgomery. I'm thinking maybe red this year. What do you think?" She doesn't wait for me to answer. "I mean, it's our senior year, so I thought school colors and all."

I want to tell Mandy that she'd look good in a burlap sack, and if she wants to wear one, I'd be happy to escort her. But I don't even get a chance to get one syllable past my lips. My pager goes off. Right on cue.

I snatch the pager off my belt. No numbers or display, just a speaker for sound. We got particular tones for certain kinds of calls—house fire, car wreck, brush fire, etc. I hold the pager up to Mandy. "Sorry, gotta go."

"Oh, yeah. No problem, Wee Wee. Time to be a hero." That could have sounded all kind of smartass, but out of her mouth, it's just nice. She jumps off the tailgate and I nearly take her damn arms off slamming it shut.

"My bad."

She waves her hand at me. "Oh, get out of here."

This is my first call, so I smack the gas a little too hard and squeal the tires in reverse. The crowd of people standing around gives a collective "Ooooooo." When I yank the gear shift into drive, I hear Thad yell, "Wait up, Wee Wee." Then he does his version of running across the parking lot.

I don't even consider waiting because it will be Christmas before Thad gets to the truck. I hit the gas and squeal out of the parking lot. Flip on my wig-wag lights so folks will get out of the way. I grab the CB mike. Cell phones are useless when dispatch needs to talk to all of us as once. "This is Tuck calling in for a twenty," I say into the mike.

Chief Griffin's wife comes back. "Hey William, we got a house fire honey, 4301 Talledega Road. Comeback." Mrs. Griffin used to be a dispatcher for the sheriff's office, but now she's retired, spending her time trying to handle the chief and our calls.

Cars on Highway 231 pull to the side of the road as I speed toward downtown. Takes about all of five seconds to get through downtown because it's barely as big as a football field. And the only occupant in the downtown square on a Friday night is Leroy Toupes, our resident wino. A half-mile later I turn off 231 onto Talledega Road. Red and white lights flash up ahead.

I park my truck a safe distance from the house—about forty yards. Three other pick-up trucks pull up behind me. I jump out, open my toolbox in the back, and pull out my gear. Had the best time in training for getting dressed out. The other guys said it was because I have a whole lot less body to work around. They meant it in a good way.

Chief Griffin and Billy Parker already got a line hooked up to the tanker. Billy grabs the hose and runs toward the house. Flames shoot out the windows on the right side of the house, but the left side is dark and still. Mr. Ehlers stands out in the front yard in his underwear, screaming, "My wife, my wife!" and waving his arms like he's the one on fire.

"William," Chief Griffin yells at me.

"Yeah, Chief?"

"Get your sawed-off butt up there and help Billy with that line. We got to get ahead of this thing."

I remember in training Chief Griffin telling me there's no use in chasing a fire; you'll lose every time.

My heart beats so fast it feels like it's going to come out my ears. I run up behind Billy and pick up the line about a foot behind him. He feels me there and looks over his shoulder. "Guess you'll get initiated good this evening."

"Looks like it."

"Well, hang on to yourself," Billy says as he holds up his hand in the air and circles it around to signal for the water.

That hose comes to life like a dragon. Even with two people holding, it fights to throw us off. I might be short, but I'm strong for my size. I wrap my right arm around the hose and lean hard into Billy. I can't see nothing but his back.

Billy shuffles forward. Water crashes into the house and roars like a tuned-up Mustang. But it's not half as loud as Mr. Ehlers screaming, "My wife, my wife!"

Seth Parker, Billy's younger brother, and Marcus Wombley run past me and Billy, going at the front door with fire axes. Seth's about the size of a wrestler on WWE, so the door might as well be toilet paper. I peek around Billy to see both of them going in. Wish it was me.

The hose starts to shove me and Billy back the closer we get to the house. "Boy, you better dig those legs in." Billy tugs forward on the hose. "Now come on."

I plant my feet and push forward. We take a few steps toward the house. The heat circles around Billy and bears into the side of my face. Skin feels like it's going peel right off. I hear Billy blow out the window with the water, and he starts filling the room. To our right Terry Brumfield and Mr. Simmons start another line on the house. Now, we can make some progress.

Seth comes out of the house carrying old Mrs. Ehlers slung over his shoulder like he's toting a deer out of the woods. She's all right though, just coughing up a storm. I turn back and try to look over Billy's shoulder to see how we're doing. Flames are gone from the roof but the room still glows so hot it's almost blue.

Me and Billy shuffle forward a couple more steps. Then there's this loud boom. Then another and another and another. Every person who has ever squeezed a trigger knows what that sound is. Shotgun.

Chief Griffin yells, "Get back. Get back now! Ammo, ammo!"

Me, Billy, Terry, and Mr. Simmons drop our lines and turn tail. About five steps away another shell goes off, and I dive, landing face-first in the grass. My helmet pops off and lands a few feet away. Three more go off. I look up. Everybody scurries behind the tanker. I crawl, stuck to the ground like a slug, as fast as I can, grabbing my helmet as I pass it.

I don't even get up. Just roll under the truck.

A few minutes go by with no more shells going off, but the fire steadily eats away at the right side of the house.

Chief Griffin figures it's safe now. He gives the command to get back to work.

We get the fire under enough control from the outside to let Seth and Marcus get a line inside. Forty-five minutes later, nothing but smoke and half a house are left.

Even though Mr. and Mrs. Ehlers just lost half of their home, it doesn't keep Chief Griffin from going nuts all over Mr. Ehlers.

"Fred, what in the hell did I tell you?" The Chief can talk that way to him because they've been in the same hunting club for decades. "Get you a fire safe. That's what I said. Been telling you for years. Could have got somebody killed out here 'cause you too damn cheap."

The Chief walks away before Mr. Ehlers can say anything back. He comes up to me and hits me on the arm. "Got your adremmal going there, didn't it boy?" He laughs, so I do too. But I'm not laughing for the same reason he is. Adremmal was supposed to be adrenaline, but the chief has got his own language, and unless you want to be washing and waxing the tanker with your own underwear, you won't mention it.

"Yes, sir, it did."

"Well, I guess it's better than algebra, but not quite as good as a woman."

"Absolutely, Chief."

"Well, come on."

We check the house for hot spots to make sure the place won't go up again. And while we do, more and more neighbors gather along the street to watch. Eventually all those watchers become carriers.

A steady stream of folks go in and out of the house, carrying furniture and stuff that can be salvaged. Poor Mrs. Ehlers just sits on the grass in her nightgown, crying over burnt photographs and busted picture frames. Guess that's why they had to go in to get her. Happens all the time Chief says.

It's about two in the morning when we finally run all the neighbors home and get the lines and gear back on the truck. I take my gear off and toss it in my toolbox. The weight of the stuff we wear is like carrying around another person on your back.

Sweet relief runs down between my shoulder blades. First fire and I didn't get me or anybody else hurt—or worse. I guess that's a blessing in itself. I should be happy. But I have to go home now.

TWO

I hear Mom before I see her—the ice cubes clinking in her glass. It's a song as familiar as "Amazing Grace" but the sound isn't even close to sweet. From the kitchen I see her head above the back of the couch, propped on her hand to keep it upright. The rest of the house is exactly like it's supposed to be at 2:20 a.m.

I could ignore her and go down the hall to my room. But she's not awake by accident. I'm sure she's already made it up in her mind that something needs to be said. What, I have no idea. We've been 'round and 'round this thing a thousand times.

"Come in here and let me see you." Her voice rings

with the same contradiction it did when I broke my arm jumping off the roof. When I was eight, I didn't understand that sound. I get it just fine now.

I drop my keys on the kitchen table and walk into the living room. Her empty glass sits on the coffee table, no bottle in sight. We never see it.

She looks up at my face and then up and down my body a couple of times, making sure all my parts are still in the right place.

"Obviously, you heard," I say.

She nods and picks up the empty glass and tries to get one more drop. "Mrs. Whitmire called. She saw the flames from down the street."

"Well, you can see I'm fine." I take a half step away, because I figure seeing me uninjured is enough to at least let this wait until daylight.

"William, one second."

We stare at each other. Her face looks like she just finished watching the saddest movie in the world.

"Why're you doing this to me?" she asks.

If it was earlier in the night, I might actually have something to say, but right now, I know there's no point in even trying to state my case all over again. "Mom, I'm really tired. Can we just talk in the morning?"

I can tell she's tired too, or maybe her glass was filled too many times. Either way, she barely nods, letting me know it's okay for me to go to my room.

When I get about halfway through the kitchen, she

says, "I just don't know why you don't love your mother."
It's the only ammunition she has left.

———

My body wants more sleep so bad it almost aches at the thought of pulling itself from the sheets and feather pillow. But my stomach vetoes any plans the rest of me might have. Frying bacon invades my room with that salty sweet smell dreams are made of. And I know scrambled eggs and Mom's biscuits are not far behind. I could lay here and ignore the vibrations in my stomach, but that would mean eating silicone eggs and bacon like used tires. Breakfast is probably the only meal not worth eating when it's left over. Not to mention how pissed Mom and Daddy get if I'm a no-show at the table. Saturday breakfast is a tradition and not something to mess with. Rest will have to come later.

I haul myself out of bed and put on the jeans I took off before falling asleep. They reek of burnt wood and rubber, but I can't be bothered with digging another pair out of the drawer.

Steven is already at the table, looking over the music he's supposed to play at tomorrow's eleven o'clock service. He's been playing the organ at the church for the past year—Ms. Inez's arthritis finally got too bad for her to keep up with the notes on the page. He begged Daddy for a chance to prove himself.

I guess he's always been doing that. At least it explains why my barely younger brother is good at almost everything.

I mean, he's like three people wrapped into one. His grades are scary perfect, he plays on both the JV and varsity baseball teams, pounds on the organ like he's possessed, and would give you his boat in a flood.

Being only thirteen months apart, it's easy for us to be allies in this house, committed to ignoring the obvious and avoiding arguments like they would trigger the rapture. We carry the family secrets like well-trained mules, and only sometimes unload our own stuff on each other. He knew way before anyone that I was going to join the volunteer fire department. Steven said, "William, that's just crazy." Then he shrugged. "But sometimes crazy is good."

I slide into the chair next to him. He drops the music he's looking at and fans the air. "Whoa, I see you brought home a souvenir. You smell terrible."

"Yeah, well, the bacon should cover it up."

"So, how was it?"

I look over at Mom standing at the stove, and then back at Steven. I shake my head, and he understands I have to tell him later.

"Guess you're working today," he says.

"Noon till six."

Steven hits a button on his cell phone sitting on the table to check the time. "At least you have the morning."

This is how we talk in front of Mom most of the time, not really revealing much of anything. It keeps everything even.

On the other side of the living room, the door to

Daddy's office opens. His Saturday ritual is to get up at five a.m., get dressed, and finish working on his sermon for Sunday. He says there's something about the peace of early morning. And he thinks this makes us kids believe that's why he sleeps in there on the sofa most nights.

"Good morning, gentlemen," he booms across the room in the voice trained behind the pulpit. I think it's funny that he always addresses Steven and me as a unit—that is, unless we've done something wrong.

"Morning," we say together, like puppets.

He sets his empty coffee mug on the table. "I see you guys made it through the night in one piece."

Daddy really just means me.

Steven nods and I say, "Yes, sir. No problem at all."

He nods, because he knows as well as I do that talking about this in front of Mom would ruin breakfast.

Daddy is a little more supportive of the whole fire department thing. I'm sure it's only because I tell him he saves people in his way, and I do it in mine. Really, what's he going to say to that?

He brings over the coffeepot he's already half-finished and fills his mug. Mom pulls the biscuits out of the oven and beats eggs in a bowl.

Daddy sits down, and we all wait to be served. It's like that in our house—not because we don't want to help. We're just not allowed. Cleaning, on the other hand, we get to do.

Within minutes, Mom has the table covered with plates, glasses, silverware, and a jug of orange juice. She seems a little unsteady, which means last night hasn't completely cleared her veins.

She sits at the round table between Daddy and me. He holds out his hands for us to join in the blessing.

"Our Kind Gracious Heavenly Father, we ask that you might bless this food, that it might go to the nourishment of our bodies and make us truly thankful for these and all the blessings of life. We ask these things in Jesus Christ's name, Amen."

The blessing is fast, the words automatic and strung together into a continuous meaningless sound. It's the same way I've heard guys at school hang up with their girl-friends, a quick loveyabye.

Mom starts passing around the food, and we all settle into the routine of a nice family breakfast, pretending that none of us notice a trace of Mom's late-night beverages still hanging around.

Generally, there are unspoken rules about what we can and can't talk about. We learned these invisible commandments as kids, and have pretty much followed them ever since we could sit up straight and eat with a fork. Church and school usually take center stage.

"So, you want to give us a sneak peek of tomorrow's message, Pastor Tucker?" I say. Daddy gets a kick out of me calling him that.

"That depends on how well you know your Bible there, Mr. Wee Wee." My nickname coming out of Daddy's mouth makes Steven laugh.

"What you got?" I challenge. This is a game we play sometimes. I've spent a lot of years memorizing scripture, partly because I like the way the words sound and partly because I've been raised by a father who believes spouting out scripture from memory is one of the pillars of a pious life.

"Matthew 25:36."

I look at Steven. "You wanna take this one?"

"All yours." Steven stopped reading the Bible or even talking about it almost two years ago. Just one of his secrets I don't mind protecting.

Daddy waits on the other side of the table while I make like I'm trying to remember. I'm just messing with him, of course.

I scratch my head and stare up at the ceiling.

"Need some help?"

"Nah, I think I got it: 'For I was hungered, and ye gave me meat; I was thirsty, and ye gave me drink; I was a stranger, and ye took me in; naked and ye clothed me.'"

Daddy claps lightly in appreciation. It's a nice moment that Mom crushes with just three words.

"Exodus 20:12."

"Connie..." Daddy says, trying to stop what Mom is starting.

She ignores him. "William? Exodus 20:12?" This is how my mom operates with religion. She highlights the parts she likes.

Even though this is the Old Testament, it's perhaps the

first scripture me and Steven learned. It's sort of a staple in the disciplinary tactics handbook in this house.

I try to make light. "Not much of a challenge there, Mom."

"Then let's hear it."

"Honor thy father and mother," I say as quickly as I can, hoping the speed of the reply will propel us off this track. But Mom won't let me off that easily.

"And..." She wants me to finish the part of the scripture most people don't bother with.

I let out a long breath. "That thy days may be long upon the land which the Lord thy God giveth thee."

Mom loves the second part of this scripture more than the first—the suggestion that you'll live longer if you do what Mom and Dad tell you. The guilt/fear combo is definitely her preferred weapon.

She looks at me. "So, you're still fine with what you're doing?"

The first time we had this discussion, I asked what exactly she thought I was doing. That really brought down the rain: *I'm not going to be one of those mothers who has to bury her child.*" *"Throw your life away.*" *"Suffering and heartache on this family.*" She went like that for about a half hour, so now I just keep my mouth shut.

"Connie..." Daddy says again. He knows this talk leads to nowhere. They have nothing to hold against me. I bought my own truck and pay for my own phone with paychecks from sacking groceries and wrangling shopping carts at the D&G. And I don't think they've bought me so much as a pair of socks besides at Christmas for two years. Mom did threaten to throw me out of the house, but we all knew she was bluffing. Not really something she would be able to keep a secret from the rest of the town.

Her eyes bounce from me to Daddy like she wants him to join in. But like the rest of us, he just wants to eat. His silent refusal to participate just pisses her off. She slams her hand down on the table hard enough to make the silverware jump. "You're supposed to honor me. That's what it says."

I slide my chair back and pick up my plate. "Mom, I guess it all depends on your definition."

THREE

If the burglars miss a few houses on Friday nights, they can make up for it on Sunday mornings. Churches dot every highway and back road all over this county, and every parking lot is full come 10:45 a.m. It doesn't matter who you are or what you've done during the week; show up for church and most folks around here will turn a blind eye. Of course blind people still talk.

Me and Thad stand on the front steps, handing out bulletins to people looking for forgiveness for Saturday night, others just needing a good song, and some who simply need their gossip fix for the week. We got all kinds.

Daddy has been giving us this duty since we were in

seventh grade. When he caught the two of us treating the fake Nativity cow like a rodeo bull, he figured the only way to keep us from tearing something apart was to keep us busy. So every week we stand at the front door greeting people.

"How you doing this morning, Ms. Mizelle?" I say and shake her cold frail hand.

"Good to see you, Mr. Franklin." Thad lightly pats his shoulder with his thick hand.

"Glad you could be with us this morning, Mr. and Mrs. Cooper," I say, while Thad hands them each a bulletin.

It's a continuous wave of smiles, handshakes, and hugs from old ladies who wrap us in a cloud of perfume and mothballs and gentlemen who didn't skimp on the Brut aftershave. Those smells are locked in my brain forever.

"Wee Wee, I'm telling you, I'm going to get carpet tunnel handing out these things." Thad loves to complain. And sometimes he tries to weasel out of this duty, but it never works. He gives in because the one thing we do have in common is that we both hate to disappoint.

"I think you mean carpal tunnel."

"Carpet, carpal? Whatever. Just keep your eyes open for Mr. Thompson."

I don't know if Thad prays much, but if he does, he's praying he won't have to greet Mr. Thompson on Sunday morning. Mr. Thompson is about six-four and about four feet wide. He's an old horse trainer with hands that feel like they've been carved out of the granite quarry over on the Georgia state line.

One Sunday a couple years back when Mr. Thompson started coming to Big Rock Baptist, Thad was the first one to greet him. Mr. Thompson stuck out his hand. Thad shook. And Mr. Thompson lost his mind.

"Boy, what in the heck you call that? That ain't how you shake a hand. You better shake a man's hand like you got a pair."

My head darted side to side to see who'd heard. Thad's face just turned as red as his clip-on tie. He couldn't say anything.

Mr. Thompson stuck out his hand again. "Now let's try that one more time."

Thad looked like he was sticking his hand into a box full of rattlesnakes. But he grabbed anyway and squeezed so hard he nearly broke a sweat. It was good enough for old Mr. Thompson. "There you go, boy. That's what I'm talking about."

But I don't see Mr. Thompson this morning. Instead, somebody just as dangerous.

Mandy and her mom come up the steps next. I hand a bulletin to Mandy, and she hugs me the way her mom has taught her to do with people they know. Thad has been known to shove me out of the way to receive this courtesy.

After all the smacks in the face with cheap perfume, Mandy's smell is as fine as a baby's hair. When she pulls back, the only thing I can think to say is, "So, did you get that dress yesterday?"

She glances over at her mom. "We did. Mom is happier about it than I am. But if I'd tried on one more, I think she would've had a coronary."

I laugh. "I'm sure whoever you go with will like it."

"Yeah, whoever that will be," she says and steps in to the church.

Her mom comes up behind her. "Hey, Wee Wee." She leans over and hugs my neck before I can give her a bulletin.

"Hey, Mrs. Pearman."

She steps back and takes the baby-blue paper from my hand. "How's your mom?" She asks the same question every time she sees me. Mom hasn't come to church much lately unless there's something special going on. Daddy doesn't say much about it, I guess because he's just as scared as me and Steven about which Mom will show up.

"Oh, she's fine."

"That's good to hear. You need to tell her to call me."

"Yes, ma'am, I will."

"And you let her know we miss her." She reaches out, pats my cheek like she's sorry for something, then gives the same smile Mandy did. This is all part of the Sunday morning pre-sermon show where some folks act like they really care because, hey, it's church and they still have to live with themselves.

As soon as they pass through the front door, Thad looks over at me and says, "Wee Wee, I don't know why you don't just go ahead and ask that girl to homecoming. You know you been dying to go out with her for forever."

"You don't know that."

"Good Jesus, it's written all over your face."

One of the ladies in the foyer clears her throat at Thad's use of Jesus. He turns and tells her sorry.

He turns back to me. "I mean, she couldn't have given you a bigger hint."

"Huh?"

"Oh, come on. She said, 'whoever that will be.' I know as much about girls as heart surgery and I even caught that one."

"Whatever." I could say more, but Mr. Thompson can handle this better than me.

"How you boys doing this morning?" His gravelly voice produces something between panic and resignation on Thad's face. Thad snaps his head over toward the steps and knows it's too late to run.

Mr. Thompson steps up to Thad like he always does and sticks out his hand.

Thad takes a deep breath and grabs his hand. He tries to look like he's not straining but the vein in his temple says otherwise.

Mr. Thompson lets go and slaps Thad on the shoulder hard enough to make his stomach jiggle. "You gettin' there, son."

He looks over at me. "Hey there boy, heard ya'll did a heck of job for the Ehlers the other night."

"You did?"

"Yeah, had to go into the feed store yesterday, and big boy's daddy here told me all about it."

Mr. Thompson is talking about the feed store Thad's dad has owned my whole life. The place serves as the hub for swapping stories for all the farmers and cattle folks around here.

"Yes, sir, I guess we did. Just wish we could have gotten there a little sooner."

"Well, don't drive yourself crazy 'bout what can't be undone." He pats my shoulder instead of shaking my hand, then steps across the threshold and takes off his cowboy hat.

Thad looks down at his crumpled hand. "That man ain't got no idea how important this thing is to my sex life."

I just laugh back at him. "Serves you right."

Steven starts up the organ inside, signaling me and Thad to shut the doors. We flip up the stoppers, shut the doors, and set the rest of the bulletins on the table at the back of the sanctuary.

We slide into our places in the back pew where just about every other kid over the age of thirteen plants for the eleven o'clock service. Daddy would like for me to get more involved with the services, but I don't have anything to offer the way Steven does.

From the first lesson Steven had when he was in second grade, he just absolutely consumed himself with practicing. He never said it, but I'm sure he did it because Mom left him alone as long as he was sitting on that bench. He would rather play the piano at church, but that's not going to happen anytime soon. Ms. Gale isn't going to let that job go until they put her in the ground.

Thad deliberately steps around Mandy so I have to sit next to her. I think he likes to torture me as much as she does. I sit down next to her even though it's not good for my soul. But what can I do?

The music fades, and Daddy's voice speaks into the mike.

"It is a beautiful morning God has given us. Amen?"

"Amen," the congregation replies in chorus.

I lift my head toward the pulpit.

"This is the perfect opportunity for all of us to take a moment and give thanks for the greatest blessing God has given us—each other."

This is different than the way he usually starts. Ms. Gale usually plays something on the piano while we all greet the people sitting around us. Guess not today.

Daddy continues. "This morning, as I look out over this congregation, I am reminded of a scripture. Matthew 25:36: 'For I was hungered, and ye gave me meat; I was thirsty, and ye gave me drink; I was a stranger, and ye took me in; naked and ye clothed me.'"

The whole sanctuary is quiet.

"Brothers and sisters, that is our calling this morning." He pauses to straighten his tie and smooth out his coat. Neither one needs it. It's one of those things Daddy does when he wants to pause to let things sink in. I've sat through hundreds of sermons and after a while, I started noticing things like that.

"As many of you know, Fred and Joy Ehlers' home nearly burned down Friday night. They lost quite a bit, and they truly need our help." He nods toward the back of the church, signaling the ushers. "Now the ushers are going to pass the plates. Give what you can. All of the proceeds will go to a fund to help Fred and Joy get back on their feet. Thank the Lord it isn't often we have to come to the aid of our brothers and sisters like this, so let's make the most of it."

He steps away from the pulpit, and right on cue, Ms. Gale strikes up "My Redeemer Lives." She always knows how to pick the song for the occasion.

Across the sanctuary I see men leaning over to get their wallets and old ladies digging in their purses. I lean over too and pull out my wallet. Grab a five and fold it once.

When the plate finally makes it to me, it's all the usher can do to keep bills from falling out on the floor.

I drop the bill into the plate. The usher presses down the pile of cash and turns to walk back to the front of the church.

Ms. Gale finishes the last verse, and Daddy steps back up to the pulpit.

"Before I ask God's blessing upon this money, I feel it necessary to recognize a few men we have here in our congregation this morning. These men sacrifice their time and even sometimes their health for all of us here in this community and they deserve our deepest gratitude. Could the men of the Coosa Creek Volunteer Fire Department please stand?"

Chief Griffin stands near the front. Then Billy Parker and, two rows behind him, Marcus Wombley and Billy's brother Seth stand. Thad reaches behind Mandy and shoves me forward. "Go on, boy."

I stand with the others. Not sure if anybody notices.

"Brothers and sisters, let's give these brave men our applause."

The sanctuary fills with hands clapping. Such a weird sound in church. Almost out of place, which is kind of the way I feel. Can't explain it. Maybe 'cause it's the first time anybody in this church has recognized me for anything other than being Pastor Tucker's son.

The congregation stops clapping, and we sit. Daddy instructs all of us to bow our heads.

I don't hear a word of his prayer. Too busy going over Friday night at the fire, trying to find something I did that would be worthy of applause. Can't think of a single thing.

I spend the entire hour with my thoughts pinging back and forth between the job I did Friday night and wondering if maybe Thad is right and Mandy was giving me a hint. By the end of the service, I've come to two conclusions: no other guy in the school could have done my job at the fire, and this is my senior year so I might as well ask Mandy, because it's not likely I'll ever get a better chance.

Daddy finishes the service exactly at noon. He knows

if he goes one minute over, people start to get all antsy in their seats. I get out before anyone else to get the doors open. I nod and tell everyone to have a nice day. Luckily, people are more worried about getting home to eat lunch than talking, so the place empties out pretty quick.

As I get the doors closed, Mandy comes up behind me and pats my back. "See you at school."

"Yeah, see you."

She gets down the steps and glides down the sidewalk. I can't help but stare.

Thad nearly knocks me down the steps. "Go on now. I know what you're thinking."

I know I have to be insane to chase her down the sidewalk, but I do it anyway.

"Hey, Mandy, I uh…"

She turns around. I look up at her. "I uh, I was just wondering. You know, since you said, that uh, well, you have a dress, but that, you know, I kind of got the impression that you don't have a date."

Her face just kind of goes blank at my rambling. But I'm in this thing now. No way of getting away from it.

"So maybe, I was thinking… well, see, would you like to go with me?" I try to say it with the same confidence I felt sitting in that pew thinking about the fire.

Mandy smiles down at me. "Oh, Wee Wee, that's so nice."

I smile back at her.

"But, really, how would we look?" She pats my arm. "Thanks anyway. You're so sweet."

I think her feet barely touch the ground as she trots her way to the car, fleeing the embarrassment I've pulled down on both of us. I just stand there looking at the ground in an attempt to locate the heart that just fell out of my ass.

Sweet sucks.

FOUR

Most people look forward to Monday about as much as getting ice in their underwear, but me and Steven find a sense of comfort in the beginning of the week. We've never really talked about it but it's something we can see in each other's faces, the way we kind of bounce out of the house in the morning. Both of us know the same thing as everybody else who grows up in a house like ours—one person's torture can be another man's refuge.

Steven is a little more upbeat than I am this morning, though. He won't be dealing with the repeated injections of humiliation I'll have to handle every time I see Mandy Pearman.

The thought makes me circle the parking lot a few times, like if I just keep the truck moving I'll spin our way into an alternate reality or something.

"William, are you lost?"

I didn't tell him what happened yesterday, so he's mystified by my driving around the lot. He wouldn't have given me hell about it or anything, but the episode still stings enough to eliminate it from topics for conversation.

"William, if you don't pick a spot, we're going to be late, and I'm going to puke if you make another circle around. Not really crazy about starting the week with either one." He puts his hand over his mouth and makes TV vomit noises.

I punch him in the arm and pull into a parking spot in the last row in the lot. I dig in my glove box to get my pager. Chief said I can't leave school for a call, but I still want to know if anything happens.

Sometimes being as short as I am is about as much fun as getting kicked in the nuts. I take that back—at least when you get hit in the nuts, the pain goes away in few minutes. There's only about two roles folks let short guys fit into: either the guinea pig or the party trick. Sometimes both at the same time. Let's just say, when you're eight years old and five guys twice your size tell you to put your tongue to a nine-volt battery at Kelly Wilson's birthday party, there's not much of a choice. The only good thing to came out of that whole thing was that I realized it's easier to hide when you can fit into small spaces.

And it comes in handy when you don't want to see Mandy Pearman before school. I creep along between cars, keeping an eye out. This might seem ridiculous. It's not like she's going to bust out laughing in my face or anything. She'd never do that. But if I know her at all, she'll go out of her way to speak to me to show how it's all really no big deal and we're still friends, and she's just forgotten the whole thing. Not really something I'm up for this morning.

I'm cruising along pretty good when Thad jumps from behind an old SUV. "HAAAAA," he yells, holding antlers on top of his head. I nearly come out of my skin.

"Watch out there, Wee Wee." He laughs and tries to catch his breath at the same time.

"Thad—Jesus, man. Scared me to death. Where in the heck did those come from?"

"Thought you was had, didn't ya?" Thad gets his stomach under control. He holds the antlers in front of me. "Look at them things, would you. One heck of a messed-up rack, but he'll eat good." The antlers on the left side are about half the size of those on the right.

"No mystery what you did after church yesterday."

"Hell yeah. I've been after this ugly guy since last year. Got to clean out the trash. Call it good game management. Heck, I probably just put this old boy out of his misery."

"I'm sure that's what you were thinking right before you let that arrow fly."

"Actually, I was thinking back straps and breakfast sausage."

"Exactly."

"Hey Steven." Thad finally acknowledges him, not that Steven would care one way or the other. For both of us, Thad is something that we kind of tolerate because he's a comfortable comic relief in our lives. "Where's your boyfriend?"

Thad says this to mess with Steven, not because he knows the truth. I'm the only one who knows that. Thad's just heard the rumors, and screwing with Steven is his way of saying he doesn't believe them.

"I guess he's in the school, Thaddeus."

Steven never protests. He lets people believe what they want. I admire him for that.

We head toward the school. Thad follows with nothing in his hands but those antlers. "I don't think those are going to be useful on Ms. Miles' test this morning," I say.

"Probably not, smart ass. These are for Mr. Price. He's helping the Fish and Wildlife folks do some study on the deer population around here."

"Still doesn't explain what you're going to do about the test."

"Heck, Wee Wee, don't you worry about me. D is for diploma. I just got to keep treating her nice. Ain't no way she's gonna fail me."

That's been Thad's philosophy since ninth grade. He talks all sweet to the teachers, runs errands for them, and acts all interested when they talk about their families or where they went to college. I swear to you, he must have set some record for the number of 70s on his report card. Then again, his ambitions don't stretch much further than taking over the feed store from his dad and spending as much time as possible in tree stand.

"Whatever, man. Come on."

Thad takes the antlers and holds them on top of his head and starts hopping back and forth from foot to foot. "D is my favorite letter. D is for deer and diploma. D is for deer and diploma."

I just have to shake my head and laugh at him. "All right Mr. Snuffleupagus, are you done?"

He drops the antlers. "Aw, going with the fat joke. Somebody pissed in your oatmeal this morning for sure. Or maybe it's that spot of blood I see."

"What are you talking about?"

"Yep, I see it right there. No doubt about it. Might want to get a bandage for that wounded pride." Thad starts laughing at his joke about the Mandy episode. If I thought he'd feel it, I'd slug him in the gut.

I just turn and keep walking, but don't get more than a step when an old blue Volvo comes screaming around the corner. The three of us jump back out of the way. The tires skirk when the car jerks into the parking spot in front of us. The diesel engine turns off, but country music still blares inside.

"I didn't know Dale Earnhardt, Jr. was coming to school this morning," Thad says, but he's not laughing.

I stare at the back of the Volvo. Stickers cover the bumper

and half the back windshield. I start reading them. *War doesn't determine who is right—just who is left. Well-behaved Women Seldom Make History.* And then the one that makes me stop. *Jesus called. He wants his religion back.*

The music turns off and the door kicks open.

Out of the Volvo climbs a girl who's five-ten if she's an inch. She's wearing Wrangler jeans, ropers, and a tank top that makes me want to drop to my knees and give thanks to God. But what really makes me stare is that she's black. Just doesn't add up.

She doesn't even look our way. She just opens the back door, reaches in, pulls out a bag and slings it over her head with the strap running diagonally across her chest. Girls will never convince me they don't do that on purpose.

"Hey sweetheart, don't let us get in your way out here," Thad says.

She slams the back door and then the front. She finally looks over at us and says, "Don't worry, I won't." It's not even close to being a joke.

She walks toward the school, and it's one of the finest sights I've seen in a while.

"You can close your mouth now, William," Steven says.

"What the hell? You believe that?" Thad says.

I got news: there's quite a list of things I find hard to believe. I guess one more won't hurt.

"Well, look at it this way. You almost didn't have to worry about taking that test," I say.

FIVE

If anybody asked, I'd have to tell them the best and worst part of living in Coosa Creek is the same identical thing—predictability. Just no getting around it. From who the girls are supposed to date to the cheese grits served with Aunt Jennie's catfish, and from the games on Friday nights to old Leroy Toupes staggering down Main Street at four o'clock on a Saturday afternoon, folks know exactly what to expect. And they definitely seem to like it just fine that way.

It's like this whole place is stuck on some big magical clock that we're all programmed into. We know where and when and what our cues are. So it throws everybody off when something—or this case, somebody—new enters our time zone.

By lunch there's already low buzz about the tall black girl that drives that blue Volvo. Thad couldn't help blabbing on and on about how she nearly killed us in the parking lot. The halls have been filled with murmurs and stares between classes. I can tell some people are already making up their minds about her. I don't pay much attention to it—just folks needing to add something to their day. All that can be confirmed is that her name is Samantha Johnson, and she's from somewhere in Iowa.

When I walk into the cafeteria after stopping by the office where Thad got sent for dipping Copenhagen in class for the umpteenth time, I see Samantha Johnson sitting at a table by herself, eating out of a plastic container and wearing headphones. I scan the room, but nobody is about to go over and tell her CD players and iPods aren't allowed at school. I'm sure it would make some folks happy if she got in trouble the first day. To them, it would help confirm the assumptions they've already made. But I try not to be one of them. Daddy has worked hard to drive into both my and Steven's heads that we should take folks the way we find them.

The line is down to about ten people, so I go to pick up my daily dose of cardboard pizza and Styrofoam French fries.

"How you today, Wee Wee?" Ms. White, who happens to be black, asks from across the steaming plastic trays.

Yeah, even the cafeteria lady calls me Wee Wee.

"Not too bad for a Monday. How you been?" I smile at her because it's impossible to talk to Ms. White and not smile. Don't know what it is.

"Just slaving away for all you kiddies."

She always says the same thing. Like I said, predictability.

"Well, we sure do thank you." I recite my line.

She hands me my tray. "You're welcome."

"Take care now," I say before moving to the cashier.

Ms. White just waves me away and stirs the mac and cheese before the top solidifies into something close to the vinyl seats in my truck. I know because I've seen guys peel off the top and sling it across the cafeteria like a Frisbee.

I hand over my $2.00 and a grab a chocolate milk out of the open refrigerator case. My body automatically starts toward the table I eat at every day, but then I can't let myself. Now, if I really wanted to pat myself on the back, I could say I walk over to her table because I remember the scripture Daddy recites to me and Steven anytime he thinks we've treated anybody wrong: *This that you do unto the least of your brethren, you do unto me. Matthew 25:41.* Truth is, no way my stomach can handle this food and Mandy Pearman at the same time today. Well, maybe it's a little of both. So just a mild pat on the back. In any case, I'd rather take my chances over here.

Samantha Johnson doesn't even look up when I set my tray on the table. Music blares from the headphones. She eats carrot sticks out of the clear plastic container and flips pages of a magazine.

Like an idiot, I clear my throat like she can hear me. Then I wave my hand close enough to her face for her to see. She looks up, no expression. I motion to ask if I can sit down. She shrugs. I'm figuring that's a "yes," so I sit.

She goes back to her magazine.

I start eating. After a few bites, it's killing me to sit right across from somebody and not at least introduce myself. Just doesn't seem right.

I pick up my napkin, wipe my hands, then stick my right hand across the table. Samantha Johnson lifts her head and then straightens her body, which puts her head several inches above mine. Just about have to tilt my head up to look at her in the eye, which you have to do when introducing yourself—according to Pastor Tucker.

She rolls her eyes and plucks the headphones off her ears. Country music blares out of them.

"How you doing? William Tucker."

She grabs my hand in a way that would make Mr. Thompson as proud as anything. "Samantha Johnson."

I'm telling you, icicles almost form on her lips, she's so cold.

"Good to meet you, Samantha."

She nods once and then grabs for the headphones.

"Hey, uh, I don't know if anybody told you, but CD players and iPods aren't allowed during school. I mean, just thought you might not want to piss off any teachers on your first day and all."

Samantha looks around the room and then back at me. She shrugs. "Thanks, William, but nobody seems to really give a shit." She puts the headphones back on, looks down, and flips another page in her magazine.

It's not often I'm left at a loss for words, but Samantha Johnson might as well have just cut my tongue out. That's about how much good it's doing me. After staring at her for a few seconds to see if maybe she'll look up, I finally give up and eat my lunch as fast as I can.

The bell rings to leave as I'm swallowing the last bite. I get up and wave my hand again at Samantha to make her look at me. "Nice eating with you," I say too loud.

At least she says, "You too" before noticing everyone leaving and shoving her magazine and container in the bag that her headphones run into.

I leave before she can get up, moving pretty quick before hypothermia sets in. Dump my tray in the trash and head to physics. And right on cue, Mandy catches me ten feet from the door.

"You didn't want to sit with us today?"

Mandy's not dumb. I'm sure she knows perfectly well why I avoided her. But if she wants to pretend, then that's fine with me. I'd like to pretend I never opened my mouth and asked her in the first place.

"Just trying to make the new girl feel welcome. You know, this isn't the easiest place to be new."

"Why do you say that?"

See, sometimes I'm smarter than I let on. Mandy's pretty easy to provoke, so any little comment will send her off on a tangent that she near about needs a GPS to get back from. And right now, any topic other than homecoming will do.

"Oh, you know. Small town, lots of little cliques and such." I push open the door and let Mandy go first. "Plus, I heard she's from Iowa so it's got to be a bit of a shock coming here."

"What's wrong with here?" Mandy spouts back.

"Hang on now. I didn't say anything was wrong. I just thought somebody should talk to her instead of staring at her from across the room."

Mandy huffs. "Not like she'd notice or care anyway."

"Still, it doesn't make it any better. What if it was you?"

Mandy doesn't even answer the question. "Well, I don't like her."

I have to laugh at that.

"What's so funny?"

"Nothing. I just figure you have to have a conversation with somebody before you decide whether you like somebody or not."

"Well, you had a conversation with her. What do you think about her? I mean, I don't really think she looks like your type."

I feel like saying that according to Mandy, she's not my type either, but I've been friends with her a long time and don't feel like doing any more damage than I've already done. So I just say, "I haven't really made up my mind yet."

"Well, maybe she'll help you make up your mind and actually hit you with the car next time."

I just shake my head.

"Who does something like that and doesn't even apologize?"

"Couldn't tell you."

"You let me know when you find out. That's *if* you want to find out."

"Look, I got to get to class."

"Okay. Well, good luck with homecoming," she says behind me in her bright little voice. That girl knows how to twist that knife once she's got it in, let me tell you.

I'm no scholar by any means, but I do like physics. And I can't think of anybody being better at teaching it than Mr. Simmons—the same Mr. Simmons who's on the volunteer fire department with us. There's no way anybody is going to get that after-lunch feeling and nod off in his class. He's always got us up doing something. Last week it was measuring speed, velocity, launch angle, and distance using one of them water balloon slingshots. We spent the whole class in the pasture behind the school shooting water balloons. Got to love a class like that. And Mr. Simmons enjoyed it as much as we did. "Twenty years of teaching and I still get a kick out of these experiments," is what he said.

When the bell rings, Mr. Simmons doesn't have to say anything. We all know the routine. There's a problem on the board for us to figure out before we get started. The first person to figure out the right answer gets points added to the next quiz. I don't want to brag or nothing, but I've racked up quite a few extra points.

The whole class flips open our notebooks and starts jotting down the problem. The only sound is pencils running across paper at a hundred miles an hour. Somebody knocks on the door.

Mr. Simmons puts down his coffee mug that hardly ever leaves his hand and walks over to the door. When he opens it, Samantha Johnson walks in. No "I'm sorry" or "Excuse me." She just hands him her schedule.

Every pencil has come to a halt.

Mr. Simmons looks over the schedule and says, "Well, young lady, looks like you found the right place." Then he looks over the room. I know it before he even says it. "You can take the seat behind Mr. Tucker there."

The seat behind me is empty because John Stringer got expelled for drinking his granddaddy's strawberry wine in the parking lot. Never liked John much, but he just scored a few points in my book.

Samantha Johnson slaps the heels of her boots against the floor and walks over to the seat behind me. She slings her bag to the floor and slides into the desk.

Mr. Simmons closes the door and looks back at the class. "Apparently none of you need these points on the next quiz," he says, prodding us all to get back to work.

I'm not even close to being done when Risa Rominger

calls from the back, "Got it." I bet none of the other males in class were close either.

Mr. Simmons walks down the aisle, takes Risa's paper, and says, "We have a winner." He marks her paper with the +5 and goes back to the front of the room.

"All right folks, clean sheet of paper. We got to get some notes down today on friction."

The class groans.

"Just bear with me. Some things just have to be done." He picks up his coffee mug with his left hand and grabs a marker with the right.

Papers rustle as the class turns to a clean page. Mr. Simmons goes to writing.

By the end of the class, we're all half-asleep with a serious case of writer's cramp. The only upside to the whole thing is that we know we won't have another day like this for a while. Notes really aren't Mr. Simmons' thing.

The bell rings. I slide back up in my seat, close my notebook, and shove it into my backpack on the floor. Me and Samantha Johnson stand at the same time. She slides by me, and I guess I can't wait for winter because I follow right behind her.

When we hit the hall, I say, "Hey, Samantha, right?"

She turns around. "Yeah?"

"Just so you know, Mr. Simmons' class normally isn't like that. We get to do some cool stuff in there."

She looks down at me and adjusts her bag. I force my

eyes to stay on her face. "That's good to hear. For a while I thought that was the class for all the insomniacs."

I laugh. "That's funny."

She doesn't even grin. "Then your standards for comedy must be pretty low. William, isn't it?"

I'm not sure whether to be insulted or not, but right now I don't care much. "Yeah," is all I say back.

"Well, William, see you tomorrow. Maybe it won't be another sleep-therapy session."

She walks away, pulling her schedule out of her back pocket.

I watch her walk away and wonder the same thing Mandy was wondering—what kind of person she is. I have no idea, but it could be a little scary.

SIX

I wish I could say that getting a job at the D&G was my idea, but I have Daddy to blame, and thank, for that. The first two years of high school I divided most afternoons between naps and clutching a TV remote. I quit football when it was obvious my lack of size and speed could in fact lead to someone rerouting my legs and/or arms up my ass. And since I don't have talents and skills like Steven, it left me floating in a field where nothing, including me, seemed to matter. I can't say it was necessarily a shit place to be. I adequately justified my routine to avoid guilt. But in our house, guilt always seems to catch up.

About a week after my sixteenth birthday, I sat with

everybody at dinner, the scraps of my nap still clinging to my face. Daddy got up from the table, went to his office, and came back with a sheet of paper. He slid it across the table to me, the words *Job Application* stretched across the top.

"What's this?"

Daddy wiped his mouth with his napkin. "Idle hands are the Devil's workshop."

I knew the point he was making. Doing nothing is just as bad as doing something wrong. I have to be right.

Even though it's way down the scale compared to putting out fires, at least there's the pleasure of regular paychecks and easy sleep after weeknight shifts—which I'm trying to enjoy when Steven sticks his head in my bedroom.

"Ouch," he says.

I roll over, still in my D&G shirt. "Huh?"

"That had to hurt." Steven loves to play with me like this—speaking like I know what he's talking about when he knows good and well I don't.

"Steven, man, I'm tired. Mess with me tomorrow."

"Shot you down cold like that, huh?"

He obviously heard at school. "Oh, yeah."

Steven comes over and lifts my shirt and looks like there's something hidden underneath. I knock his hand away. "What are you doing?"

"I just want to see if she left a mark."

"Get the hell out of here," I say too loud.

"William," Mom calls from the living room. I swear she has deer ears.

"Well, if it makes you feel any better, at least you did something and got shot down instead of doing nothing and wondering about it forever."

"I think forever might be stretching it."

"Oh whatever. You've lusted after that girl since before I remember. That's why I'm saying, had to hurt."

"Wasn't fun, let me tell you."

"So, who is plan B?"

I roll back over and shove my head into the pillow. "Don't have one."

Steven shuts my door. "You better get one. I need you to double with me and Buck."

My eyes pop open and I bolt upright. "Excuse me?"

Steven smiles. "Yep, talked him into it."

"Then let me talk you out of it."

"Can't be done. I've made up my mind. Everybody knows anyway."

"They don't *know* know.

"Might as well."

Talking Steven out of something of a "principle" matter is about like ramming your head against a brick wall, so I don't even bother. "You know this could be ugly."

"Yeah, that's why I need you to go—might have to put out a couple fires for me." He laughs.

I fall back on the pillow. "What about Mom and Daddy?"

"What about them? They got to find out sooner or later. I mean, I'm not going to really say anything. I figure word will get back like it always does. And if they have a problem, they'll say something. If they don't, then it won't be any different than now."

I shake my head back and forth because I know the shit storm this could cause. My instincts, which Chief Griffins says I should always follow, tell me to say whatever it takes to keep Steven from making a colossal screw-up. But he's excited.

Steven takes the world head-on, whereas I feel more comfortable chasing after it. He likes to make a mess. I clean it up.

The only thought in my head is the second half of a scripture that's always reminded me of Steven: " ... that no man put a stumbling block or an occasion to fall in his brother's way." And I'm definitely not going to now.

"All right, I'll find somebody."

SEVEN

Even though the food is bad enough to make a buzzard wince, lunch at school is valuable time—time I didn't know was so important until now, as I step away from the cashier and realize I just can't sit with those people anymore. Whether they actually are or not, all I'll be able to think about is them making fun of me for even thinking I had a chance with Mandy. They would never say anything, but that's sort of worse than just coming right out with it. At least I won't have to worry about that sitting with Ms. Johnson.

Samantha sits at the same table with her headphones

on. I walk over to the table, but I don't ask to sit this time. I just do it.

She looks up at me from her magazine. I say "Hey," even though there's no way she hears me over the music blaring into her ears.

She flips the headphones off her head and stares at me. "You know, you don't have to sit here." She looks around the cafeteria at all the other tables with empty chairs. "Wouldn't you rather sit with your people?"

"What do you mean, *my people*?" I ask, even though I know what she means.

"You know what I'm talking about. Take a look at the tables in here. Don't you see a pattern?"

Samantha is referring to the line that's always existed in this school, in this town. There aren't but about twenty-five black students in the whole school, and they always sit together without a white face among them.

"Well, what about you?"

"I obviously don't have any people here. Not too many black cowgirls from what I can see."

"That's your problem. Maybe what you think you see isn't really what's there."

I expect Samantha to storm back at me, but I don't care. I filter what I say too much anyway.

"Yeah, maybe." She closes her magazine, reaches in her bag and turns off the CD player, and leans on her elbows on the table. "But what's the deal anyway?"

"What do you mean?" I take a bite of my hamburger.

"I mean, are you some kind of social leper around here? Or are you some kind of Good Samaritan who feels like he has to save every poor lonely soul? Got to be one of those."

"Neither. I just want to eat my lunch in peace. And you seemed pretty distracted." My eyes involuntarily dart toward my regular table, where they're watching.

Samantha looks over her shoulder and sees them too. "Oh, I get it. Trying to piss off your girlfriend."

"She's not my girlfriend," I say and take another bite.

"So that's why you look like hell. You two have a fight?"

"Thanks. Not why I look like this." I can't really say, "I tossed and turned all night because my gay brother wants to come out at the homecoming dance."

Samantha stays on the same train of thought. "Did she tell you that you don't give her enough attention, or did she give you the I-don't-like-you-hanging-out-with-your-friends-so-much speech?"

Samantha's assumption pisses me off. "Look, you want to give it a rest? What's your problem anyway?" I glare at her for second. "Take a look. Do girls like that go out with guys like me? Damn, I thought you were smart."

She looks at me for a few seconds, surprised but almost pleased.

"Hey, look, sorry. I just don't want to be somebody's charity case," she says, in a voice totally different from everything else she's said.

"I don't think you have to worry about that around here."

"That's good to hear. Last thing I need is some of these country girls inviting me over for the Sunday lynching." She pops a carrot in her mouth and shakes her head.

"Hey, this might be Alabama, but it's not like that around here."

"Fair enough, Will," she says, using a name nobody has ever called me. It's always the full William or Wee Wee. I kind of like the way it sounds coming out of her mouth, minus the piss and vinegar. "And what'd you mean, guys like you?"

Even though she asks like she really means it, I just can't get into it. No point. Can't change reality. It just is. "Nothing. I's just spouting off."

We both finish our lunches in silence. Samantha doesn't put her headphones back on or open her magazine. It's not much, but at least it's some indication she cares enough not to act like I'm not here.

When the bell rings, I grab my tray and stand up. She whips her bag over her shoulder.

"See you in physics," I say.

"Yeah, see you there."

———

You know a class is going to be a little unusual when the teacher stands outside the room dressed like a caveman. Mr. Simmons obviously hasn't done this with his other classes because no way word wouldn't have got passed around like John Stringer's homemade strawberry wine in the Winn-Dixie parking lot.

He stands at the door wearing some one-piece leopard-print outfit with a messed-up black wig on his head and what looks like homemade flip-flops on his feet. The leopard fabric only covers one shoulder, so Mr. Simmons has a T-shirt underneath—I'm sure to hide the caveman-like hair that sticks out of the neck of the shirt. In his left hand he's holding a papier-mâché club instead of his coffee mug. I stop at the door.

"Mr. Simmons? Or should I call you Mr. Flintstone?"

He plays along. "Today, William, either one will do." He smiles and hits me in the arm with his club. "Now take your seats."

Mr. Simmons stands in the doorway until the whole class makes it in. Everybody pauses at the door to give him a strange look, but he stays in character, simply motioning his head to keep them moving.

When the bell rings, Mr. Simmons steps into the room. "Today, class, we are continuing our study of friction. But to properly study its effects, we're going back a few thousand years." He turns off the lights, walks over to the counter in front of the whiteboard, and turns on his laptop and the LCD projector. An illustration of a primitive man pops up on the whiteboard.

"Now, in prehistoric times, perhaps nothing was more essential to the survival of man than the discovery of fire. It provided light, warmth, a way to cook food, protection—all provided through the proper use of friction."

Mr. Simmons reaches over and hits a button on the computer. A video window pops up. "Today, thousands of years later, man—and woman for that matter—still use the same principles in survival situations."

The video starts. It's a pair of hands hovering over a pile of what looks to be wood shavings.

"Here a survival expert shows the proper technique for using a flint to start a fire."

We all watch in silence as the pair of hands uses a piece of metal to scrape against the flint to throw sparks down on the wood shavings. After five or six strokes, the sparks catch, and the hands gently place some small twigs on top of the shavings. Within seconds, it's a real fire.

The video stops, and Mr. Simmons flips on the lights. "Now, how many of you would survive with no matches, lighters, or a magnifying glass?" He pauses to see if anyone is brave enough to answer. "Well, today we're going to find out."

He points to the back of the room. "On the table in the back you'll find some paper sacks. In each one you'll find some instructions and a ball of lint, courtesy of three weeks' laundry at the Simmons abode. It won't look like much, but in all the things I've read about starting a fire, they say this is the best way. You'll also find some twigs, and a flint with a metal scraper attached. I want you to pair yourselves up, grab one sack, and follow me."

He makes a move toward the door, but nobody budges. Mr. Simmons looks back at us and says, "Let's go, Homo sapiens."

This makes a couple of idiots laugh, but we all get up and head for the table.

"I know lunch was no picnic, but you with me on this?" I ask Samantha.

"Sure, as long as you don't set me on fire."

"Don't worry, I know how to put you out."

Samantha grabs the brown paper sack off the table and we walk out into the hallway where Mr. Simmons points toward the door at the end of the hallway with his club. "Out the back, around the horticulture trailer. You'll see some fire rings set up. Sit next to one and wait for me."

Next to the dozen fire rings, I find Chief Griffin with the brush-fire truck. He sees me and comes over. "William, are you part of this whole circus?"

"Yes, sir."

"Well, thank the Lord. At least I'll have a helping hand in case one of these nitwits decides to burn the place down. Jerry must have lost his ever-loving mind with this scheme. Hell, I thought he was joking when he called me."

"Chief, Mr. Simmons never jokes about his experiments."

"Guess not. But don't you worry. Got the hose ready to go."

I look over to the brush-fire truck and see the hose already unrolled and lying on the ground.

Chief Griffin takes off his hat and says, "William, who do we have here?" He's looking at Samantha.

"Oh, sorry. Samantha, this is Chief Griffin."

He sticks out his hand. Samantha takes it and shakes.

"Heck of a grip there for a pretty lady." Chief would flirt with Medusa if she was standing next to me.

"Who said I was a lady?" Samantha says, smiling.

Chief Griffin lets go and laughs. "Watch out, William, you got a tough one there."

"Chief, we're just classmates."

"Mmm hmm. William, you can dry that one out and fertilize this whole field."

Samantha laughs.

"Anyway, Chief, we need to get to a station."

"Ya'll go ahead and get your learning done."

We walk over and kneel down by a fire ring made with bricks that look like they should be on somebody's house. I'm sure Mr. Simmons got them donated, like he does just about everything else for our experiments.

He walks behind the last pair, Nikki Macalusso and DJ Trahan. DJ's name isn't really DJ, and those aren't his initials either. He wants to be a DJ for a famous rapper someday, so he goes a little beyond just dressing the part. He's kind of a joke around here. But from the look on Nikki's face, she doesn't think it's very funny getting stuck with him.

With everybody in place, Mr. Simmons paces around the circle of fire rings. "Now before I let you open your bags and read the instructions, everybody, ladies and gentlemen included, make sure you don't have any loose clothing hanging. Guys, tuck those shirts in and roll your sleeves up if you got them."

For most of us, this is a pretty easy task. But DJ fights like a rat caught in a sleeping bag with his oversized T-shirt that about five of me could fit in. He finally gets most of it tucked down in his pants.

Mr. Simmons holds a stopwatch up in the air. "All right, let's see how long it takes. How many of you could survive? Ready? Go."

Samantha opens the bag, takes out the instructions, and holds them out for me to take. I look at her like she's kidding.

"Excuse you, Neanderthal man. So the girl can't build a fire?"

I don't have time to fight with her, not that I would want to even if I did. So I take the sheet of paper. I look around at the circles, and I'm the only guy holding the instructions. Figures.

I start reading. "First, make a small nest with the twigs."

Samantha pulls out the handful of twigs and starts assembling the nest in the middle of the fire ring. I just have to take the opportunity to get her back a little. "See there, you know who's giving the orders around here."

She glares up at me.

"Kidding."

She finishes the nest. "Next?"

"Place the lint in the middle of the nest."

Samantha takes out the dusty multicolored ball in a flash and places it in the appropriate spot.

"Okay, come on. Let's go. We got to be first," she says.

"All right, hang on." I look down at the instructions and read. "Now here is where you need some muscle. Don't be bashful. Hold the flint just above the cloth and strike the flint hard to create enough sparks to catch the lint."

Samantha takes out the flint and holds it over the nest of twigs.

I keep reading. "Watch your hands. These are sparks you're dealing with."

"Yeah, yeah, I hear you."

"No, that's not me. Mr. Simmons wrote it here."

Samantha gets ready to hit the flint.

"Hang on. When the lint catches a spark, pick up the nest, making sure to hold it in front of your face so smoke doesn't get in your eyes. Blow gently. When the twigs start to catch, place the nest back in the fire ring. Good job. You're a survivor!"

Samantha looks at me. "Can I do this now?"

"Go ahead, Pocahontas."

Samantha starts striking the flint with fury. Sparks fly into the ring. It doesn't take but a few strikes before it catches. She slowly picks up the nest, holds it a few inches in front of her mouth, and blows. In a matter of seconds, the twigs catch. She places the bundle back in the fire ring and yells, "Fire."

A split second later, DJ yells the same thing. But his isn't in the ring. It's in his lap.

He dropped the twigs in his lap, and now his shirt is on fire.

"Roll, roll, roll!" I jump up off the ground and run over to DJ, grab his shoulders, and sling him to the ground. "Roll, roll."

DJ starts rolling, but the flames catch the dry grass instead of going out. I yell, "Chief!"

Chief Griffin runs, as much as he's able, over to the brush-fire truck.

The flames grow on DJ's shirt. He tries to beat them out with his hands.

I run over to Mr. Simmons. I don't even bother asking. I just grab the top of his leopard-print outfit and yank it over his head, leaving him standing there in his T-shirt and boxers.

By the time I get back to DJ, almost his whole T-shirt is engulfed. I spread out the leopard fabric and dive on top of him to smother the flames. He's screaming, but I stay on top of him until I know the flames are out.

I pull the fabric off. Only singed scraps of DJ's shirt are left, and he's really burned up.

Chief Griffin starts spraying the ground so the fire doesn't spread.

Everyone stands with wide eyes, silent. Some take small steps backward like the fire that got DJ is going to come after them. Mr. Simmons, in his boxers and T-shirt, starts yelling, "A phone, somebody give me a phone!"

Nobody moves for a second. "NOW!"

A few people fumble in the pockets to produce a phone. Mr. Simmons snatches the one closest to him.

DJ writhes on the ground in pain.

"Just keep still, DJ, keep still. We'll get somebody here for you."

He looks up at me with real fear in his eyes. I stare right back, caught, like I'm being pulled into a cave.

"Wee Wee, it hurts."

"I know it does. But you got to keep still."

He stops moving, but keeps moaning. His arms shake back and forth.

"Everybody inside," Mr. Simmons yells, but nobody moves. "NOW."

The rest of the class start to make their way to the building. DJ tries to turn his head to look.

"Keep your eyes on me," I tell him.

He looks back up at me. "Wee Wee, my mom."

"Somebody will get her, don't worry." As soon as I say it I know that might be easier said than done. Everybody knows who DJ's mom is, even if nobody says it. She's been a lot of teenage guys' first, and some married men's only, but that didn't keep their wives from leaving anyway.

"What is she going to do?" he says, in that way like he thinks he's not going to be here to find out.

"Man, don't worry about that. Everything's going to get taken care of." I know the words don't mean anything.

DJ coughs a couple times but keeps talking. "You know, Wee Wee, I got a job. At the Garden Center. Nine bucks an hour."

"That's great." I look toward the highway because I can hear the ambulance in the distance.

"Yeah, told my mom she could stop, you know? I could give her my paychecks."

I have no right to hear this. These are words for people who've earned them. I feel like somebody dropped a rock on top of my head.

DJ looks at me like he wants me to understand so bad that he'd set himself on fire again just to make it happen. So I nod. "Yeah, man, I know." And I guess in some way, I do.

He squeezes his eyes shut, the pain wrapping around him without mercy. The only thing I can do is talk to him to take his mind off of it. "DJ—hey man, hey." I snap my fingers to bring him back to me. "I know you want to be famous, but don't you think this is a bit much. Heck, I don't even get the twenty-five dollars for this call." I smile at him, and he does his best to smile back.

"Just hang in there. We'll get you out of here and fixed up in no time."

DJ nods.

Moments later the ambulance comes screaming around the school and out onto the grass. Principal Edwards has made it out of the building. He's standing with Mr. Simmons, who hangs his head, too scared to look over at DJ I guess.

When the EMTs make it over, I stand up and get out of their way. "DJ, you're going to be fine, man, just fine."

"Thanks, Wee Wee," he barely squeaks out.

"Just doing my job."

The EMTs work fast, and I can't take my eyes off a single move they make. I feel tangled in all of this. The fear that I should have felt a few minutes ago comes creeping up my spine. My hands start to shake a little, and I just pray with all I got that DJ will be okay, that my work wasn't in vain.

When they lift the gurney and start rolling DJ toward the ambulance, I finally take a deep breath. I'm the only person left except for the Chief, who's fighting the hose back onto the brush-fire truck. So I go to help him.

"Well, for a little guy, you're a big hero today," Chief says. "You saved that boy's life."

All I can say is, "Yeah, I guess I did."

"Feels good, don't it?"

"I don't really know." I pause, replaying what really just happened in my head. "Guess it's freaking me out a little."

"That's all right, as long as that happens afterward."

"So you think he's going to be all right?"

"Yeah, I suppose. I've seen much worse folks pull through. But you can't worry about that now. You did what you's supposed to. You start second-guessing and it'll drive you stark crazy. You hear me?"

"Yes, sir." I hear him.

EIGHT

"Just tell me what you saw, William." Mr. Edwards peers at me from across his desk. I didn't even get a chance to sit down in my last class before the intercom clicked on and called me to the office. Should have seen that coming.

"Fire, sir, that's what I saw. One second everything is going fine, the next DJ, I mean Paul, is screaming."

Mr. Edwards nods and writes on a yellow legal pad. "And what did you think about the instructions for the assignment?" He picks up a copy just like the one in our paper sacks, glances at it, and then hands it over to me. "Do you notice anything that maybe should have been included in the instructions that might have prevented this? Seeing as how you're a trained fireman."

"Volunteer fireman, Mr. Edwards," I say, because I can tell he's fishing—looking for something specific to blame all this on. I don't want him thinking I'm some kind of real authority or anything. I just put them out when I see them. "Might be better for you to talk to the Chief."

"We've already taken Chief Griffin's and Mr. Simmons' statements, William. I just want to make sure everything matches up."

"Everything here is pretty straightforward. Clear. Not really any room for confusion." I suddenly get the feeling like I need to say something that will keep Mr. Simmons out of trouble. "I mean, these flint kits are sold in every outdoor store from Alaska to the Appalachians. Folks use them every day without incident."

Mr. Edwards continues to jot stuff down on his notepad. He stops, sets the pen down, and then finally asks the only question he really wants answered. "William, do you think there is anything Mr. Simmons could have done that would have prevented this? Or is there anything he didn't do that led to it?"

"Can't really say. Guess sometimes you just got to factor in the randomness of the universe. Some stuff happens while some things don't."

"Well, I don't know how much that's going to comfort Paul's mother."

I can tell he's annoyed, and I kind of am too because

he's all like he wants to find some way to pin this down on Mr. Simmons. "Sir, the way I look at it is, it's not something we can really help. The truth sometimes is everything but comfortable."

Mr. Edwards looks at me like he knows I'm right but wishes I wasn't. I know it sucks being in the position he's in, with folks wanting answers followed by apologies and policies that will keep everybody safe all the time. If that was the case, then they wouldn't need me. And I'm kind of glad they do.

Finally, Mr. Edwards leans over on the desk and writes me a pass back to class. "William, you're a sharp young man."

"Thank you, sir. I try."

———

When the bell does finally ring I get out of the school as fast as I can because the whole place buzzes like a hornet's nest about what happened. I make it to the parking lot to see Steven waiting for me at the truck, and I also notice Samantha—who's treating her Volvo like a punching bag.

I don't know if it's possible to put a human fist through the hood of a car, but from the looks of it, Samantha Johnson is bound and determined to find out.

People and cars file through the parking lot without even giving her a glance while she pounds the faded blue hood with everything she has. So I figure I better stop her before there's nothing left, of her hand or the car.

"Hey hey, hang on there, Tex."

She stops banging and glares up at me. "WHAT?"

I hold up my hands in surrender. "Hey, hang on. What's the problem?"

"You mean besides the collective IQ of this hick-ass town?"

"Yeah, I guess," is all I'm brave enough to say.

Samantha straightens her tall brown frame. Her chest heaves with deep breaths. "This," she says, and points down at her tires.

I walk around to the passenger side of the car. Both tires are flat.

"Some redneck's idea of a joke," she says, getting control of herself.

"Nah, not a joke."

"No shit."

"I mean, if it was a joke, they would've got just one tire."

Samantha kicks the front tire. "Dammit."

"Guess you need a ride, huh?"

She looks at me, her breathing close to normal. "No, Will, don't worry about it. I'll just call my dad. He's probably out of class." She picks her bag up from the ground where she laid it before the assault on the poor Volvo. She reaches in and takes out a cell phone.

"Really, it's no big deal," I say to stop her.

"Really, you should let the hero take you home." Steven walks up and puts his arm around my shoulders.

Samantha looks at the phone, back at me, and then at Steven, her eyes still sharp as razors.

"Samantha, this is Steven, my brother."

She composes herself a little. "Hey, sorry about the theatrics."

"Don't be. That's the best fight I've seen around here in a long time." Steven flashes his super-wide smile that disarms every person he meets.

Samantha almost laughs. "Yeah, well, I'm sure that's not the case."

"Well, sweetheart, I sure wouldn't mess with you." Steven is the only guy I know who can get away with calling girls sweetheart and not get an earful.

I turn toward Steven. "I guess you heard, huh?"

"Yeah, just crazy. How bad was it?"

"Pretty bad."

Steven nods. "Not really up for talking about it, huh?"

"Nah, it's fine. My head's just not really around the whole thing yet. Still kind of like the whole scenario is disconnected from me. But I'm sure it will settle in at some point."

"Will was pretty much like an action hero—minus the muscles and digital animation," Samantha says.

"Oh, Lord, don't say that." Steven shakes his head. "He'll start working out like a lunatic now."

They both chuckle.

"Whatever," I say.

We all just kind of stand there not knowing who's

supposed to say what until Samantha pipes up. "So, you're brothers, huh? Which one is adopted?"

We smile at the same time. Nobody would ever guess Steven and me are related without knowing us since we were in diapers. He's tall. I'm short. He's got sort of long brown hair, and I don't have much hair at all. I'm more of a jeans and T-shirt kind of guy, and Steven puts way too much thought into what he wears.

"Yeah, yeah," is all I say.

"Well, hey, Samantha, it was nice meeting you." Steven looks over at her Volvo. "You, uh, made quite an impression." He starts to walk away.

"Hey, you're not riding home?"

"Nah, me and Buck are going over to the batting cages. Baseball season might be way off, but he doesn't want to get stuck on JV again this year." He walks backwards, away from us. "See there, we *are* brothers. Both just trying to do what we can for our fellow man." He shoots that smile over at Samantha. "I'll see you around."

"See you later," she says.

I look over at Samantha. "Come on, I can get you home."

"You sure? I mean, I'll give you some money for gas."

"No need. Let's go." This is simply the product of being a pastor's son.

Samantha checks the doors of her car to make sure they're locked, not that anybody could steal the thing. But some things are just habit, I guess. Then we both walk across the parking lot toward my truck. And all those people who didn't even look her way while she was freaking out all over her hood are sure taking some notice now.

Some slow down and stare through their windshields. Others stand outside their cars with the keys hanging in the door. They look surprised, but they shouldn't. They know what kind of guy I am.

I don't pay them any mind. Like my daddy's said too many times, sometimes you just have to do what's right, even if nobody else thinks so.

I unlock her side first and open the door. After she climbs in, I shut it and throw my backpack into the truck bed. As soon as I get in, I notice how high her knees are because the seat is shoved up so far.

"Sorry it's so cramped. I can't reach the pedals otherwise." I kind of laugh.

"Yeah, well, I guess both of our legs cause some problems."

"But I'm sure it's not as many as your fists do."

Samantha smiles and looks down, then rubs her hand. "Yeah, I'm paying for that now."

As I pull out of the parking spot, people still stare. Samantha notices.

"I'm sure you'll have some explaining to do tomorrow."

Even though I know what she means, I pretend otherwise. "Don't know what you're talking about."

"Right," is all she says back.

"Which way?" I ask when I pull up to the highway.

"Oh, sorry. Left."

Out on the highway, Samantha points at the little black box with the red switch mounted on the bottom of the dash. "What's that?"

"Wig-wags."

"Wig-what?"

"It's a switch that makes my headlights blink back and forth. Remember, I'm a volunteer fireman. We all got them, you know, for when we go to fires."

"Wouldn't a red light be better?"

"I guess, but only official government vehicles can have those. And there's nothing too official about a beat-up Chevy."

"So, Will the Fireman, what's it like? I mean, being a big hero?" she asks with just a drop of vinegar. "Is it fun? Guess it would have to be, to volunteer for it."

"I don't know if 'fun' would be the word I would use."

"How come?"

"Okay, maybe it is. It's tough, though."

"I like tough."

"I'm not surprised."

Samantha doesn't respond, which gives me a second to contemplate our little exchange. I don't really trust my judgment on these matters, but I'd swear she was kind of sending me a message there. And even though I try to hold my moments of humiliation down to at least one a week,

I think I might have just found plan B. She's definitely got the backbone for the assignment.

"So, where we going?"

"You know where Smoke Rise is?"

"Yeah, just off Highway 231 a few miles south of downtown."

"That's where I live. Well, my mom and dad and me."

"Nice neighborhood."

"If you say so."

"What? You don't like it?"

"I liked our property in Iowa a lot better. We had horses. I used to run barrels. Was pretty good at it too. I liked racing against the clock."

"That explains it."

"What?"

"Your wardrobe."

She looks down at her Wranglers and boots. "I know. Not much need for these anymore, but it's still who I am."

"So what brought ya'll down here?"

"My dad is from down here. He wanted to come back. So when he got offered a teaching position at AUM, he took it without even asking my mom and me."

I take the next right and start heading through downtown. We get stopped by the only traffic light. Samantha looks out the window and sees Leroy Toupes sitting against the old auto parts store that had to close up when Auto Zone came to town. Now the building just waits for a bulldozer or a natural disaster. "Look at that poor guy."

"Yeah, that's Leroy."

"Looks pretty rough."

"He should. He's been wandering around here for years. If he catches you on the street, he'll tell you it's his birthday and ask for money for food."

"That's sad."

"I know, but what do you do?"

As soon as I ask the question, Samantha reaches in her bag and pulls out her wallet and takes out some dollar bills. She gets out of the truck before I can stop her and walks over to Leroy. She hands him the bills and says something to him. Leroy just looks up at her like she might be a figment of his imagination.

The light turns green, but I can't go. Samantha jogs back to the truck and gets in.

"What did you say to him?"

"Happy Birthday."

I pull away. Samantha stares back at old Leroy.

"That was nice of you, but he'll probably buy liquor with the money," I say.

She shrugs. "That's his decision. I can only do what I can do."

The only thought that comes into my head is, "I like this person." But in a way I'm not used to. Can't hardly explain, so I won't try.

"What are you going to do about your car?" I ask her.

"I don't know. I guess get a couple of tires and get it home tomorrow. I can't just leave it there in the parking lot."

"No, you can't. And I don't think you should let it stay there tonight. I know a guy who can help you out."

"Why shouldn't I leave it up there tonight?"

"Well, let's just say I'll bet good money your back windshield won't make it through the night."

"You think?"

"Oh yeah. Folks around here feel pretty passionate about a few things—God, the South, and country. In that order. Some of your stickers might spark the wrong flame, if you know what I mean."

"Guess I didn't think about that. But if they're pissing somebody off, then they're doing their job."

"Why would you *want* to piss people off? Hell, I spend a good bit of my day trying to do the opposite."

"I don't know. I just like letting people know where I stand."

Before I can respond, she blurts out, "So what do *you* think about them?"

I'm not about to fall into that trap. Samantha Johnson isn't the only smart one in this truck.

"Doesn't matter. It's not my car."

"Well, I like them. They make people think."

"Let's just hope it's not about where they should put the baseball bat."

She laughs a little and says, "Anyway."

We make it to the Smoke Rise subdivision without much else to say. As soon as I drive past the sign, I ask, "What's your address?"

"Oh, 1222 Briarcliff."

"Know exactly where you mean."

I take the next left onto Briarcliff. "You got a pen and paper?"

"Yeah. What for?"

"Take this down. This is a guy who can help with your car."

Samantha reaches into her bag and rummages around for a pen and a scrap piece of paper. "Okay, go ahead."

"Guy's name is Leonard. He tows cars, sells used tires and such. His number is 567-8667. Just tell him you know me, but don't say Will. He won't know who the heck you're talking about. Just tell him you know Wee Wee." It almost kills me to say it.

"Wee Wee?" She barely stifles her laugh.

"Yeah, yeah, I know."

"Thanks," she says, putting the cap back on her pen.

I pull into her driveway. As soon as I do, a tall white man comes out the front door.

I stare.

"My dad," Samantha says.

"Oh. Well, yeah, I kind of figured."

"Kind of throws some people off, you know. Anyway, I appreciate the ride, and the number. Not used to people doing me favors."

"That's just 'cause you don't know people like me."

"I think that's pretty safe to say, with the whole jumping on top of fire and stuff."

Samantha starts to shut the door, but I stop her. "If it'll make you feel any better, I'll let you do a favor for me."

She gets this look like she knew there had to be something.

"Homecoming. Will you go with me?"

She smirks and shakes her head, then gazes into the air like she's trying to piece some things together in her head. The silence is killing me, after the Mandy Pearman disaster. Finally she says, "Sure. With some conditions."

"And what are those?"

"I'll let you know at some point. But don't worry, it won't hurt too bad."

"Right."

NINE

I've always liked my job at the D&G, even if it's another example Daddy can point to as proof of his wisdom. It's easy, not much thinking involved. Bag the groceries, stock the shelves, round up shopping carts in the parking lot. But today I wish it would at least keep me from wondering how DJ is doing. Guess it's something every firefighter has to deal with.

With about an hour left on my shift, Daddy comes walking through the automatic doors, dressed in a shirt and tie. Not normal for a Tuesday night.

"Daddy, you didn't have to get all dressed up just to come to the D&G."

"Oh, don't get all excited thinking this is for you. I'm going down to the hospital to see Paul—to pray for him. Lord knows he needs it, and I don't know who else is going to do it."

"You hear how he's doing?"

Daddy's face gets real serious. "Just that he's got third-degree burns on his arms and most of his torso."

"Yeah, I figured."

"William, I just thank the Lord you were there, son."

I have no way of responding to that. That's about as close to Daddy saying he's proud of me as it gets. He's just always expected me and Steven to do the right thing. It's not something that has to be praised, just what we're supposed to do.

I can only nod. Such a strange feeling swirls around inside of me that I can't hardly make sense of it, knowing that if just one small factor had been out of place, then Daddy would be preparing for a funeral instead of a hospital visit. And I am that factor. It makes the ends of my fingers tingle.

"Thought maybe you'd like to go down with me."

The first thought that jumps into my head is the Chief telling me I should never visit victims in the hospital or go to their funerals. "Now you listen to what I'm saying. You don't need to be bringing that kind of shit with you on calls," he said.

"Well, I still got an hour left on my shift."

"I can talk to Mr. Whitehead. I'm sure he'll let you go early, given the circumstances."

I know I should refuse, just follow what Chief said to do because he's pretty much been right about everything else when it comes to fires. But I just don't feel right saying no, like I can't be bothered. I guess it might help if I could explain to Daddy why I shouldn't go, but it's not something he'd understand. He'd just look at me the way he does when he's disappointed. So I say, "Okay."

Daddy walks over to the customer service counter and talks to Mr. Whitehead, the manager. Mr. Whitehead nods and they shake hands. Daddy comes over and says, "No problem at all."

I'm immediately aggravated with myself for letting Daddy kind of control me like a puppet, like he knew I really didn't have a choice in the matter. I'm sure he'd pretty much decided before he even left the house that this would go like he wanted, like most everything else. Not much I can do about it now though, so I say, "Let me clock out. I'll meet you in the parking lot."

When we get in the truck, I have to ask. "So, did you talk to Mom?"

"I did indeed."

"And ... "

"And she's the one who told me I should go down to see Paul," he says, avoiding what I'm really asking.

"Huh."

I guess maybe I shouldn't be surprised. When I was too

little to know not to talk about it, I asked Daddy why Mom kept that glass with her all the time. I can still hear his answer as clear as an October sky. "Son, your mama has got her finger on the pulse of a lot of suffering. She feels it beating all the time." I figure he deliberately gave me an answer I wouldn't understand to keep me from asking again. But it's never kept me from pondering his reply.

———

The one thing Chief Griffin nor anybody else could train me to handle is somebody's mother crying at just the sight of me walking into a room.

Daddy and me walk into the hospital room where DJ lies on the bed—shirtless, swollen, and covered in a thick white gel that looks like homemade Vaseline. Ms. Trahan sits at the side of the bed with her head resting on the rail, like she's beat Daddy to the praying.

She hears our steps on the white tile floor and looks up. Tears spill down her face.

It's the worst sort of crying—the kind that pours like it's coming out the end of a hose but doesn't make a sound. Something about the hurt and fear is so bad it makes the world go mute.

If it weren't for the blanket of hard years that drapes over every inch of Ms. Trahan, somebody would swear she's young enough to be DJ's sister. They share the same eyes, nose, and slight frame. But her skin looks like she's had too many cigarettes and not enough sleep.

She gets up out of the chair, walks over, and throws her arms around me. Her head buries into my shoulder, shaking with sobs. I have no idea what to do or say. I just take one hand and pat her back.

Daddy doesn't say anything either. I figure with as many hospital rooms as he's had to walk into like this, he'd have something. But he stands there with his hands crossed in front of him, looking at the floor like he's embarrassed.

Eventually, Ms. Trahan lets go, steps back a little, and stares at me with her red eyes that are swollen almost as bad as DJ's arms. "God bless you, Wee Wee," she says.

I have no response.

Daddy saves me from thinking of anything to say. "Ms. Trahan, we just wanted to come by to have a word of prayer for Paul." He says this in a low voice, like he's worried about disturbing the air in the room.

Ms. Trahan takes a step toward Daddy with both arms extended, and he quickly holds up his hands to stop her. "If you please, we're just here for Paul."

She stops. Her back stiffens at Daddy's refusal, but then she nods without surprise or blame. I guess she's used to be people putting her off.

It isn't that easy for me. Brick walls have a softer touch than he does, and I just can't look at him right now.

Daddy shuffles over and stands next to the bed. He flips open his Bible, turning page after page, hesitating but never stopping. The thin, almost transparent pages rustle as he fingers the corners, then snaps them over. I watch him staring down at the scripture, trying to find something, words that will be good enough for DJ.

I can't help but think of what he should read for himself.

Daddy makes it all the way to 2 Corinthians before he stops, grabs a handful of pages, and turns the book back to the Old Testament. A few more pages and he finally stops turning. He clears his throat and reads: "'So do not fear, for I am with you; do not be dismayed, for I am your God. I will help you; I will uphold you with my righteous right hand. Isaiah 41:10.'"

He closes the book and bows his head. So do Ms. Trahan and I.

He prays for God's guidance for the doctors, his strength and comfort for DJ, and, of course, forgiveness for the sins of the parents. I love my daddy, but sometimes I'm surprised we share the same blood.

When he says, "Amen," Ms. Trahan steps over and covers my right hand with both of hers. "Wee Wee, I want you to understand something. I want you to look at my boy there." She stops so I can turn my head. "Air is going in and out of him because of you." She squeezes my hand tight. "A little while ago, the doctor came in here to tell me what they're going to have to do. He went on about pain, medication, skin grafts, and procedures. In all of what he said, there was only one word I really heard." She stops just long enough to look at me, to make sure I'm really hearing her. "Recovery."

She smiles. "He's going to be fine, eventually."

All I can do is nod and say, "That's good to hear."

TEN

"Your father says Paul is lucky." Mom's body fills the bath-room doorway.

I look up from rinsing the toothpaste out of my mouth. "That's one way to put it." I wipe my mouth on the towel, then move forward to show her I'm ready to go to bed, but Mom doesn't budge.

"Sit down a minute."

My shoulders fall and arms hang loose. "Mom, right now?"

"Yeah, right now."

I plop down on the toilet like I'm about to have my

mouth washed out with soap—which, by the way, doesn't work in case any future parents want to know.

"When you were little, this was the only room in the house small enough to get you penned up." She half smiles, remembering the times she chased me with the fly swatter. "Guess some things always stay the same."

"No kidding," I say flatly, my eyes dropping to the glass in her hand.

Mom ignores my comeback. Her glass goes on the counter and she sits on the edge of the tub. "So, tell me."

"What? The fire?"

"God, of course not. You want to kill me? The hospital, Paul. How's Debbie holding up?" She says his mom's name like they've been friends for years.

"Uh, didn't you already do all this with Daddy?"

"I'm not doing this for me. I'm doing this for you."

"For me? Mom, I was kind of there. I've got the play-by-play in my head."

"Tell me how it felt to see Paul like that. His mother."

I know my mom wants me to say it scared me to death. She wants the chance to tell me that's how I'm going to end up. But that's not the truth.

"I was happy, Mom—glad I was there. Just think for a second. If DJ, or me, was in any other class, then he might be in the morgue instead of a hospital bed. You know what Daddy would say about that."

"I do. But sometimes I'm not sure how much your father believes what he says."

"What's that supposed to mean?"

She ignores my question. "What about Debbie? Do you want me in a hospital room like that?"

"Mom, that's a dumb question."

"What do you think are the odds?"

"Actually, if I don't do something severely stupid, then pretty good. Look at the Chief. Forty years and not a scratch on him."

"I'm sure that's not the norm, William."

"Well, I'm not the norm either."

With that, Mom just nods, picks up her glass, and walks out of the bathroom. Before I can get up and get out, she steps back into the doorway. "William, I'm going to get some things together for Debbie, if you'll take them down to the hospital for me tomorrow."

"Sure," I say without question. I know one place my mother never wants to go back to is a hospital.

ELEVEN

"You're psychotic." This is what I tell Samantha about her jacked-up idea of sitting in the parking lot on the hood of her car watching people walk into the school. She thinks she'll be able to tell who slashed her tires just by looking at them. Even though the whole thing probably saved her dad money in the long run—Leonard took a few days to tackle some other issues with her car—she's pissed and feeling like a victim.

"I'll know as soon as I see their face," she says. "People's faces don't lie, Will."

"You know, the FBI or CIA would probably be pretty interested in this so-called ability of yours."

"Just wait. Plus, I've got to let people know they don't scare me."

"Oh, so now we're getting down to it. This doesn't have a thing to do with finding out who messed up your tires."

"Will, in this world, you have to stand up and be seen or people will run right over you. That's one thing my mom has been driving into my head my whole life."

"Well, I think she might have caused some brain damage in the process."

"Oh, whatever, Will. You know, you don't *have* to sit here."

"I'm committed to people's safety."

"Ha Ha."

We sit while people stream in from the parking lot and off buses. Most people try to act like they don't see us. I can see how they're forcing their eyes forward. Even Thad goes by without a nod in my direction. I don't blame him much. He's too wrapped up in trying to put holes in deer to try to make sense out of what I'm doing.

I watch Samantha watching them. She has a nice face, which is easy to miss with the kind of physical presence she has and how much her mouth gets in the way. I wouldn't call her pretty or hot, but I find myself a bit captivated. Maybe that's better than pretty.

"Will, would you stop staring at me?" Samantha says without looking at me. "I'm concentrating."

Before I can say anything back, I hear, "Wee Wee, I know you want to buy one."

"Mandy," I say like I've been caught digging through her purse or something. "Heeey."

She holds out a handful of orange rubber bracelets with the letters *S O S* on them. "Come on, Wee Wee, you have to get one. It's only a dollar."

It's already been pretty much carved in granite that I'm locked in the friend zone when it comes to Mandy, but I can't help feeling like I don't want her to think I'm "with" Samantha. Stupid maybe, but the truth sometimes doesn't make any sense.

I scoot away from Samantha and look at the bracelets. "So, what's *S O S?*"

Mandy smiles big like it's just the question she wanted me to ask. "Students Offer Support. Indians in Action are selling them to raise money for ... "

"DJ," I finish for her.

I'm not surprised. I thought I only saved DJ's life. But it looks like I've given him a new one. Over the past few days, the halls of the school have become plastered with posters for DJ, some with well-wishing messages, others asking for donations for his medical expenses. Jars in local stores and gas stations have been put out for the same reason. The IIA (Indians in Action) Club has cooked meals and delivered them to his mom. The local newspaper even has an article every day tracking his progress, rehashing the incident. Students who either ignored him or made fun of him have even gathered around the flagpole in the morning to pray for him. So maybe the fire wasn't a tragedy, but a gift.

It's like the same spark that set his shirt ablaze also scorched people's memories. I'm happy for him. Like my daddy says from the pulpit, everybody deserves a chance to start again.

"Yeah. So you want five of them, right?" Mandy says, laughing.

"Well," I say, reaching back for my wallet.

"I think Will has done enough, wouldn't you say?" Samantha chimes in and grabs my arm.

Mandy almost staggers back. "Uh, excuse me?"

"Oh, you know, he kind of saved his life and all. I'd say that's a bit more than digging up a dollar for cheap plastic."

Uh-oh. I swear, if this was a science fiction movie, this would be the part where the special effects folks would add spewing bile or magical spikes shooting from Samantha's eyes.

Mandy is speechless—and gorgeous. Not really the time to notice, but I do. And I almost feel sorry for her, unknowingly walking into the buzz saw that's Samantha Johnson.

"I think she's just trying to help out," I tell Samantha, trying to hold the line between defensive and polite.

"Right," Mandy says. "We're just raising money for DJ. Poor guy. You know, that's kind of what people around here do. They help each other."

Samantha nods like she appreciates Mandy's pissy-ness. "Then why the bracelets? Why not just ask for the money?"

"The bracelet is just a way, I don't know, to show

everybody we're being supportive. Kind of like bringing everyone together." Mandy straightens her shoulders.

"Ah," Samantha says. "I think we'll pass." She doesn't move her hand from my arm, keeping me from pulling out my wallet.

Mandy looks at me like I'm suddenly not good enough to be on her team. I guess she never really saw me anyway.

"Thanks, though," I say.

Mandy stands there for a second. She cuts her eyes at Samantha and then at me. "Wee Wee, I thought you were bigger than this."

"But not big enough for you to go to homecoming with, right?" Samantha must be rubbing off on me.

Mandy smirks and kind of lifts one eyebrow. "When I'm right, I'm right." She waves with her fingers. "See you."

A mixture of anger and embarrassment churn in my gut. I turn to Samantha. "Let me try and understand this. You give money to a drunk like Leroy, but not to help out DJ."

"Who said I wouldn't?"

"In case you blacked out the past five minutes, you've just kind of missed the opportunity."

"Will, that wasn't about helping DJ. That was about making themselves look good."

"I'd say she's doing a pretty good job then."

"Will, you really don't want to have anything to do with her."

"I don't?"

"Nah. Some people just don't see things the way they should." Samantha puts her arm around my shoulders.

"Well, maybe she will one day."

"One can always hope."

And some people can help.

Mandy, the bracelets, the surge in support for DJ. They make me remember a Psalm: *You make the winds your messengers, fire and flame your ministers. —Psalm 104:4.*

TWELVE

On a Friday night it almost isn't worth turning on the lights at the D&G. Early in the evening, the place is busy with mamas picking up Hamburger Helper and pancake mix for Saturday morning, and daddies grabbing cases of Natural Light to make it through the weekend. But it all comes to a screeching halt at seven thirty, about the time the Coosa Creek Indians kick off.

The only good thing I can say about it is, it means I don't have to work myself into too much of a sweat before the shift ends and I have to be around other people. Nothing a clean shirt and a squirt of cologne can't fix.

At the end of the night I make one more trip out back

to the Dumpster and see the wooden pallets stacked high. They rarely get piled like this because people steal them for bonfires on the weekend. I guess folks have been holding out for homecoming.

If Chief Griffin saw this, he'd definitely say it's a fire hazard. I could tell Mr. Whitehead, but I need a fire tonight, the same way Steven has to practice his music before Sunday morning.

I finish unloading the trash into the Dumpster and get back inside to help Misty Jenkins wipe down the conveyor belts before we close up. The fluorescent lights and elevator music make the place creepy when it's empty, like some scene in a horror movie. But the only ghost I see is coming through the door. It's Mr. Simmons.

I haven't seen him since he was standing outside the school in his boxers. Word is he got suspended, pending a hearing with the school board. If DJ was given a new life, then Mr. Simmons looks like his has been taken away. His face is pale under several days of not shaving, and if his shoulders hung any lower, his knuckles would drag on the ground.

He sees me.

"William." He half waves. "Just a couple things the missus forgot to pick up. I'll be out of your way in no time."

I want to ask how he's been, but that would be a stupid question. Instead I say, "Class ain't the same without you."

"Might start getting used to it," he says without looking in my direction.

By the time Mr. Simmons makes it back to the check-out,

I've worked up the courage to ask him what everybody in class wants to know. "So, when are you going to be back?"

His mouth does this smirk that shows both confusion and pain. "You're guess is as good as mine." He rubs his stubbled chin. "Don't know if I will be back."

My eyes get big. "What? You kidding?"

He can't say a thing, so he just shakes his head.

"But it was an accident."

"Yeah, but I created the situation that caused the accident. I should have been more careful. I'm responsible for the safety of all my students at all times. Or at least I'm sure that's the way they see it."

I stand there looking at him, trying to grasp the idea that one messed-up experiment could ruin all the great stuff he's done leading up to it.

"Look, Wee Wee, it'll be all right," he says, not even coming close to being convincing. "There's a school board hearing coming up at some point. We'll get all this sorted out."

Yeah, I get the feeling they're going to sort him right out of school.

"But don't worry about any of that. Just keep putting out fires."

"What about you?"

"Well." He pauses to rub the side of his face, obviously searching for the right words. "Let's just say I'm not really feeling up to it right now." He forces a grin. "But don't you worry about me."

He doesn't know I can't help it. I worry about everybody.

═══════

"I guess you're just begging for it, aren't you?" I say to Samantha after she tears into the Winn-Dixie parking lot, making people jump out of the way before they end up a hood ornament. This is one of her conditions for going to homecoming with me. Must be seen in public together before the actual event. Something about testing the waters. I don't know.

Samantha steps out of the car. "What? Oh, my driving? Well, you're here to save anybody who isn't paying attention."

"Not if they have a Volvo stuck up their ass."

"Ooo, Will, nice sarcasm," she says like she's pleasantly surprised. "But it doesn't suit you. That's my job."

She ignores the comments bouncing around the regularly assembled parking lot crowd: "What's her problem?" "Bitch going to kill somebody." "Why don't you slow down?"

So I do too.

Samantha slings her bag over her shoulder, then pulls out a newspaper and tosses it to me. "It says there's going to be a school board thing about Mr. Simmons and the whole DJ incident."

"Yeah, already got the news straight from the horse's mouth."

"What? You talked to him?"

"He came into the store tonight. Looked pretty rough."

"No shit. I can't imagine." She plops on the tailgate next to me and scans the parking lot. "So, this is it?"

"It?"

"The battlefield."

"Nooooo. Par—king—lot," I say like I'm talking to a toddler.

"Yes, I know that, dipshit. We had a place like this in Iowa. It was an abandoned rest stop instead of a parking lot. Served the same purpose, though. You know, a place to see who has the coolest car, the newest clothes, who's hooking up with who. Everybody trying to get one-up on somebody."

"I guess. Hadn't really thought about it."

"You better."

"So what was your one-up?" I know she had to have one. Samantha just has that vibe.

She smiles at me like she knew I'd ask. "Making the most people shit their pants."

"I think you might have done that here too."

"Ah, that was Sesame Street stuff. Last year, Halloween, I rigged up this costume that made it look like I didn't have a head, but I could still see. The rest stop was only about three miles from my house, so I rode over on my horse and came galloping through everybody like in *Sleepy*

Hollow. People went everywhere like I'd dropped a grenade or something." Samantha smiles big and blazing, with the kind of joy I don't see often.

"Sounds pretty funny."

"Yeah, some people even had nightmares." She's only slightly proud of herself.

I chuckle at the thought of her with no head storming through a crowd of people on horseback. But my laughter doesn't last. About four spots away, Buck and Steven are getting out of Buck's dad's truck. "Speaking of nightmares."

"Oh, good, they came." Samantha hops off the tailgate and goes toward them. They stand by their truck like it's a life raft.

"What? You told them to come out tonight?" She ignores me.

Steven has always known what lines not to cross. Both of us have made keeping the peace a lifelong study. So he's got to know he's crossing a line now. People around here like their rumors as long as they stay rumors. That's why the few times he's come out here, he's come only with me.

Ordinarily, two guys showing up in the same vehicle wouldn't be a big deal. But most guys don't have the trail of murmurs and speculations spread out behind them like Steven and Buck. I guess maybe I thought Steven's idea about homecoming was just talk. But I should have remembered Steven doesn't say much he doesn't mean.

Samantha walks them over toward me. I can't help but

take a few glances at people. The stares have started. Girls smile. Guys grimace.

Steven grins uncomfortably. "Hey, William. Samantha suggested we come out and test the waters, you know, before tomorrow night." He says this knowing good and damn well what I was going to ask.

I feel like I've been tricked. "You couldn't clue me in on this?" I ask Samantha.

"Nope. You would've talked him out of it."

"You don't know that."

"Okay, maybe I didn't *know*. But I had a pretty good idea."

"Anyway," Steven jumps in. "Doesn't matter. We're here now."

I take a look at Buck. He looks like he's going to puke in the bed of my truck. "Hey man, you going to make it?"

He nods, like if he talks somebody will all of a sudden notice he's here.

Steven looks around the crowd. People pretend they weren't just staring, but at least no one looks like they're going to blitz him.

"See?" He places his hand on Buck's shoulder. "This isn't so bad."

"Not yet," I say.

"Don't pay any attention to him, Steven. He's just scared."

Samantha is right. I might as well be wearing yellow

feathers and shooting eggs out my ass. I won't deny it, even if I do hate it.

"And I'm not the only one with some sense." I motion toward Buck, whose face is slowly turning from pale to green.

"Whoa," Samantha says. "Why don't the two of you sit down." She sits in the middle of the tailgate to make them sandwich her. She puts her arms around them like she's known both forever.

"Did I go through some kind of time warp or something?" I ask. "Or didn't ya'll just meet like a few days ago?"

"Kindred spirits," Samantha spouts, before either Steven or Buck has a chance to answer. Then again, Buck doesn't look like he wants to participate in any of this.

The whole thing makes me look down at my pager and pray that it will go off.

A fire would be so good right now.

THIRTEEN

The only cars in front of the D&G now are the ones parked by the highway with *For Sale* and a phone number written in white shoe polish on the front windshield. The green numbers on the radio say 3:16. I smile because it makes me think of John and that some things have to be done for the greater good. Not that a pile of wood is much of a sacrifice.

I drive past the parking lot because there are too many lights, and even though the likelihood someone will drive by and see my truck is pretty slim this time of night, I can't take a chance. Just like Chief Griffin says, you got to think ahead of the fire so you can keep control. *"No sense in chasing after it because you'll never catch it."*

I park my truck in the used car lot about a hundred yards away from the store, where it won't look out of place. A drainage ditch runs along the edge of a brush area that goes all the way behind the D&G, so I walk in it to stay out of sight.

The back of the store is lit with a floodlight. It isn't hard to see. I dig a couple of cardboard boxes out of the Dumpster and tear them into small pieces. You can almost make this stuff burn by rubbing it between your fingers.

I pile the pieces in the middle of the bottom pallet and take a matchbook out of my pocket. I strike one and light the corner of a piece of cardboard. Now I just have to wait.

There's nothing wrong with this. These pallets would be taken and burned anyway. The only negative is that someone's plans for a homecoming bonfire will get ruined. But this is more important.

I take a few steps back from the stack and watch. The small ball of orange grows and grabs the wood with its warm fingers. Within a couple of minutes the wood transforms into a column of flames. It's such a nice sight. It's doing just what I want.

And the sound is amazing. Pops, crackles, and the air-rushing whoosh of the fire consuming its food is better than any song I've heard. This is my song. And I'm playing it well.

The flames climb to about twenty feet and smoke billows into the dark sky. I move closer to the fire because I have to. I soak the heat into my skin, proving I don't have to be afraid. I'm not going to end up like DJ because I've got this under control.

The top pallets finally catch, and the flames grow so high they top the building. No doubt they can be seen from the highway. And that's a good thing. The situation is well in hand. So I walk away.

Just as if I made the call myself, my pager goes off as I get back to my truck. But I wait to hear the sirens.

When I hear them in the distance, I crank my truck and pull out of the used car lot. I ease down the highway below the speed limit, trying to time this just right.

The tanker pulls into the parking with screeching tires, no doubt driven by Seth Parker. I'm sure the Chief is cussing him the whole time. I'm the first one to pull behind the store. Seth and the Chief are pulling a line off the truck. I change into my gear.

I don't even ask. I just grab the end of the hose and run toward my fire. Can't let anyone else put this out.

When they get the line hooked up to the tanker, I give the signal. My feet slide on the sand and gravel on the asphalt, but this thing is not going to beat me. I lean hard into the pressure. Some of the burning pallets fall against the building. But there's no chance of the concrete wall going up. This fire's not near that hot.

Wish Mandy could see this.

In about half the time it took for the flames to migrate through the boards, cracks, and stacks, I have it down to a black smoldering pile. And the back wall of the D&G is barely discolored. I'll probably even volunteer to clean it for Mr. Whitehead.

Seth shuts down the hose. I drop it about the same time Marcus Wombley pulls up and gets out of his truck. I can't help it. I have to yell, "Snooze, you lose."

The Chief takes off his helmet and shakes his head. "Hell, I don't even know why I put all this crap on. Seth, we could've sat back and had a cup of coffee."

"Man, I was getting some good sleep," Seth says. "But at least I won't have to hear the wife fuss about the way I smell when I climb back in bed."

"William—good Lord, son, you got here fast."

I just shrug.

Chief Griffin looks over at Marcus. "Well, better late than never. We'll let you situate that line back on the truck so you at least get credit for the call."

Marcus isn't happy. "Don't you think that's Wee Wee's job?" he asks the Chief.

"Hell, he's done the hard part. You don't even have to dress out." The Chief laughs a little.

Marcus knows arguing with Chief Griffin always turns out to be a lesson in futility, so he starts pulling the hose back toward the truck.

Chief walks over, puts his hand on my shoulder, and looks at the pile of ashes. "Well, that's one less field we'll have to worry about them kids burning up this weekend." At least once every football season, somebody's bonfire gets a bit too big and turns into a full-on brush fire. "I know I'll sleep better."

"Me too," I say.

FOURTEEN

There aren't many occasions that require me to wear a coat and tie. Maybe a couple times a year—dances, weddings, and funerals. And tonight, it feels like I'm going to the last one instead of the first. After surviving last night without incident, Steven is downright giddy about the dance. I'm not sure if he gets that his presence last night was just a hint, rather than the hit over the head it will be when he and Buck walk into that gym. He's about to seriously disrupt the order of how people like it around here, and he couldn't be happier about it. I love my brother, but he scares me sometimes.

I finish getting my red tie on and grab my navy blue

sport coat. Steven is putting on finishing touches in the bathroom. Every hair looks like it's been drawn into place. He's wearing blue pants and a khaki sport coat, the exact opposite of me. His tie is something I would never pick out. I couldn't describe it if I tried.

"So, what do you think?" he asks.

"It's different."

"That's the whole idea, isn't it? Kind of a theme I'm building."

"How'd you get the clothes?"

"Are you kidding? Dad's credit card almost jumped out of his wallet when I told him I had a date for the homecoming dance. You know, minus the identity and gender."

"So, you didn't tell them?"

"No. I thought about it. But I just didn't feel like having a fight today."

"And let's hope we don't get one."

"Amen," Steven says. He tightens and straightens his tie one last time, and I hear Samantha honk the horn in the driveway. It only took about thirty minutes of pleading and altering the truth to convince her not to come to the door.

She was all like, "What? Are you ashamed of me?"

It was hard to make her see that wasn't the case, but years of practice helped.

The house is silent when we walk through the kitchen and living room to the front door. Daddy is at the church practicing his sermon for tomorrow. Mom hides in her room because she's all pissed that our dates aren't coming over for pictures. We told her we were meeting them there. All of us know why we don't have dates come to the house, but it still doesn't keep her from fighting us tooth and nail about it.

"Mom, we're gone," Steven yells into the house. She doesn't reply, not that I expect her to. This is a sad house sometimes.

When we get in the car, Samantha says to me, "Ready for a nice evening, senator?"

"What?"

"I mean, with that red tie and blue coat, you look like a delegate for the Republican National Convention." She laughs a little.

"Thanks." I look her up and down, with her low-cut blue dress, hair up, and makeup, to find a comeback. She looks like a whole other person. Amazing. But I have to give her one anyway. "Excuse me, but I thought I was going with Samantha Johnson. Do you know where she is?"

"Ha ha," Samantha says, smiling, and throws the car into reverse. Steven half falls into the front seat.

"Jesus, sweetheart, does William have to go to a fire?"

Samantha just looks down at Steven wedged in between the seats and tells him how good he looks. He returns the favor through grunts as he dislodges himself.

"Let me call Buck and tell him we're on our way."

Samantha stops at the end of our driveway that's really like a road. "Which way am I going?"

I point toward town.

"Hey, yeah, we'll be there in a few minutes. You ready?" Steven says.

I can hear Buck's voice coming out of the phone, and whatever he's saying it's not a simple yes or no.

"What? Are you kidding me? Don't be like this."

Buck's voice barks back.

"You can't let people scare you off. Are you going to hide forever?"

Samantha looks over at me and mouths, "Drama."

"Well, we're coming to get you anyway. So get dressed. Or not. Whatever you want." Steven shuts the phone without saying good-bye.

"Problem?" Samantha says.

"Yeah, Buck doesn't want to go. He's worried we'll be like chum in shark-infested waters."

I shrug. "Well, you can't make him go."

"Yes, I can. Plus, he'll thank me later."

Steven leans forward and tells Samantha where to turn to get to Buck's house. He has to hang on to my headrest to keep from getting slung around. He grunts, pulls, and pushes. "Girl, I'm going to be seasick by the time we get there."

"Huh?" Samantha says like she's completely lost on the whole idea that she's about to sling us into the ditch.

"Take the next right, and then it will be the fourth house."

When Samantha gets to Buck's road, she comes almost to a dead stop before turning. I'm not kidding—I could push the car faster. When she straightens the steering wheel, she says, "Was that okay for you old ladies?" and laughs.

"Anyway," is all I say.

Steven knocks on the door, but nobody comes to let him in. He knocks two more times before barging in. He doesn't even bother shutting the door. A couple of minutes go by.

"What do you think is going on?" Samantha asks.

"I won't be surprised if Steven has Buck in a headlock, dragging him down the hall."

Samantha laughs. "Get out of here."

"I'm serious. Stubbornness is a dominant family trait."

But when Steven comes out, he doesn't have Buck's head locked under his arm. Instead, he's got an armful of clothes with Buck running behind him in his boxers.

Steven opens the car door and dives in. Buck runs up to the car. "Dammit Steven, give me my clothes. I'm not going." The poor boy looks like a four-year-old who just got his toy stolen.

Steven looks up at him. "All right. If that's what you want." He opens his arms and drops the clothes and shoes on the seat. Buck leans into the car to pick them up. Then Steven grabs both of his arms and jerks him through the back door. "Hit the gas," he yells at Samantha, which is like telling a thoroughbred, "Giddy-up."

Samantha shoots out of Buck's driveway with the back door still open. We're a hundred yards from the house before Buck finally closes it. He looks over at Steven after shutting the door and says, "You just got to have your way, don't you?"

"Yep."

Buck gets dressed in the back seat while Samantha drives us to the Ox Yoke, a steak place out on Highway 231. There's a few other couples dressed in their homecoming duds, but they pretty much ignore us. Buck pouts through the whole meal, and Steven lets him. He doesn't even try to make him feel better about this whole thing.

When the two checks come, I nearly have to jump out of my seat to keep Samantha from grabbing the little black book from the server. She starts to protest, but I hold up my hand and say, "No arguing. If I let you pay, they'll never let me back in here."

Samantha twists her mouth as if to say, "Whatever."

"Thank you," I say.

Steven pays for the meals too. Buck's nervousness has kind of infected all of us so we don't say much. We just get in the car and head toward the school.

There's a stream of couples flowing toward the front entrance. Girls in short dresses and heels they'll wear only long enough to take pictures and then their shoes will end up piled in the corner somewhere. I've been to enough dances to know.

We all get out of the car and look at each other. Steven smiles big at everybody and says, "Well, ya'll ready for this?"

FIFTEEN

It's almost like we're invisible when we walk into the dance. Nobody looks, waves, or even acknowledges that we're here. Of course, I guess the opposite would be worse.

Steven grabs Buck's arm and says, "Hey, let's go ahead and get our picture taken before the line gets too long." Then he looks over at me and Samantha. "Ya'll coming?"

"Absolutely," Samantha says.

When we get in line, I take out my wallet and pull out a twenty.

"What do you think you're doing?" Samantha asks.

I look at her like this is a stupid question. "Uh, getting money for pictures."

"No, sir. You got away with dinner. But I got this." She actually reaches two fingers inside the top of her dress and pulls some bills out of her bra. It's kind of trashy, if you ask me, but that doesn't keep a light shock of electricity from shooting through my business. And my eyes nearly fall out on the floor.

"What?" Samantha says. "It's not like this dress has pockets or anything."

"Ever heard of a purse?"

She just shakes her head. "Getting in this dress was enough. I couldn't bring myself to carry a purse too."

I look at Steven. "Can you believe her?"

He just smiles because he knows I got my hands full.

The line grows behind us, nearly reaching all the way back to the entrance, which is no surprise. This picture is apparently the most important part of the evening. Everybody needs to show their parents evidence that they actually showed up, I guess. Even though this thing lasts until eleven o'clock, the dance will be nearly cleared out by nine thirty. Here's how it goes: pictures, a couple of dances, say hey and hang out for a little while to justify buying the dress and going to dinner, and then it's off to a party. Trevor Wombley, Marcus's younger brother, is the host this year. Or maybe I should say the victim. Come Monday, there will be as much talk about the aftermath as the party itself.

The line inches forward with Steven and Buck in front of me and Samantha. The beat from the music hits so hard that it almost messes up all the hundred-dollar hairdos.

Girls lightly push back pieces of hair and make last-second adjustments before they enter the lights.

The photographer's set-up is the only bright spot in the room. Those finished taking pictures stand off to the side, forming a bit of a crowd, to watch their friends and make comments to make them laugh.

By the time Steven and Buck are next, the crowd has reached mob status. And Steven looks quite satisfied. This is the audience he wants. He knows that when he and Buck get in front of the backdrop and adopt the same pose as all the other couples, the rumors will stop. Won't be any more guessing, wondering, and speculating by anybody. The truth is on display for everyone.

The flash goes off, and the photographer yells, "Thank you. Next."

Steven grabs Buck's hand and leads him over to the backdrop. Buck looks like a dog being led to the little room at the back of the pound. But he knows he has no choice. If he fights it, Steven will just make a bigger scene.

The photographer doesn't even hesitate. He slings his ponytail back over his shoulder and arranges Steven and Buck in the same position as everyone else. Steven stands behind because he's taller. Even over the music, I can hear yells from the mass of people.

"Faggots."

"Rump Ranger."

"Fudge Packer."

Steven doesn't even look in their direction, no matter

how bad it gets. People behind us laugh, whisper, and make their own jokes. Usually, folks have watched their tongues about Steven when I've been around, but this opportunity is obviously too good. Too many of them and not enough of me.

I look up at Samantha, half-expecting her to turn around and tie someone's tongue around their forehead. She only shakes her head and says, "Assholes."

After their picture is taken, I make a move to run over in front of both of them to escort them past the mob. But Samantha grabs my arm. "Will, you can't."

She's wrong. I could. Luckily I don't have to. When Buck and Steven get close, the crowd scurries away like this is a remake of *Invasion of the Body Snatchers*. Except they're laughing.

The only thing good I can say is at least it takes the attention off me and Samantha. To some folks, the two of us together is as bad as Steven and Buck.

Samantha pays the photographer with her bra money, and we take our place. I put my left hand on her hip like all the guys do. Of course, she towers above me, so I don't look or feel as casual as I'm supposed to.

"No standing on your toes back there," she says.

"Are you kidding? I need stilts."

We both laugh just as the drumbeat shakes my insides and the flash goes off.

"That picture's gonna be funny," Steven says when we

step out of the light and into the dark of the dance. "Make sure I get one."

I punch him in the arm. "It's not like I can help it."

"Me neither, my little brother. Me neither." He smiles and rubs his arm.

The four of us stand there looking at each other with that uncomfortable confusion about what the hell we do next. There's not much choice—dance floor or go sit around one of the tables along the walls.

"So, ya'll want to sit down?"

"Not really," Samantha says.

"It's a dance. If I wanted to sit down, I could've stayed at home and watched TV," Steven jumps in.

I look at Buck, and he has the same face I do. Neither one of us want to go near the dance floor. And I'm sure it's for the same reason: I don't want to die from embarrassment, and Buck doesn't want to die from blunt-force trauma to the head. He knows they can only push their luck so far. So I decide to save us both.

"Ya'll two go ahead. We'll get a spot at a table before they're all filled."

Samantha's not the least bit disappointed, which does kind of sting a little. But not enough to make me change my mind.

She grabs Steven's hand and they head for the red and blue lights flashing from the d.j. stand.

With Buck following me, I walk toward the line of tables. Halfway over, I take off my jacket and fold it over my arm. I barely get ahold of it before two big arms bear hug me and lift me clear off the ground.

"Hey there boy, looking pretty spiffy tonight." Thad laughs and shakes me up and down.

"Could you put me down before my dinner ends up on the floor?" I yell over the music. Thad has done this since we were little kids, and I've always hated it. He knows I hate it. It's like I'm some kind of toy to be tossed around.

He drops me. I spin around just in time to get a beer burp right in the face. This explains this sudden affection even though he's kind of steered clear the last week or so. Thad's a friendly guy, and even more so when he's raided his dad's stash in the garage.

"I see you've gotten into the blue gills tonight." Blue gills are Busch Lights, but that's what Thad's dad calls them because he only drinks them when he's fishing on the Coosa.

"Well, you know. It *is* my last homecoming. My dad's gonna be pissed when he checks his fridge out in his workshop. But hey, what do you do? I got some out in the truck if you're in need."

"Nah, don't worry about it."

"Yeah, I know you, Wee Wee. Always got to be the good little boy."

"Whatever, man. Hey, you know Buck."

Buck half waves at Thad, who only nods back at him. It's about what I expect. Thad is not mean enough to be blatantly shitty, but he's not going to be fake, either.

I finally take a good look at what Thad is wearing—Mossy Oak camo pants, a white, short-sleeved button-up shirt and a camo tie that matches his pants. "Dude, what are you wearing?"

"Wee Wee, this is the nicest thing I got. Hell, these pants hadn't even been in the woods one time."

"I guess I shouldn't expect anything else."

"Plus, it ain't what I'm wearing you need to take a look at," Thad says. "Have you seen Mandy?"

"Nope, haven't had the pleasure yet."

"Pleasure is exactly what it is. And pain too, I guess, for all us poor unworthy souls. She looks finer than corn-bread and butterbeans."

Thad barely gets the words out of his mouth before I see Mandy and Brett Toler walking our way. I glance to my right to see that Buck has walked off and found a place at a table by himself. I'm sure he feels safer in the shadows.

The only thing shining brighter than Mandy's red dress is the grin plastered across her face. She's got her arm all tucked around Brett's, strutting like she's in front of a hundred cameras. Thad was right, though. If her dress was any shorter on the bottom or lower on the top, they would have never let her in the door. That's one of the things that pisses me off about her. She knows exactly how to push it right to the line without going over it. Makes me nuts.

"Hey, Wee Wee." Mandy takes her free arm and wraps it around my neck, pulling me way closer to Brett Toler than I'd ever like to be. She smells like my childhood before

Mom switched to gin. Actually, I can smell it on both of them.

She lets go, and I take a step back. "I guess ya'll brought Mr. Daniels out with you tonight."

Mandy looks at me funny. "Who?"

I raise my eyebrows. "Jack."

It actually takes a second for it to register with either one of them.

"Oh, ha ha." She moves a piece of hair out of her face. "Just a little."

I'm sort of surprised, but I really shouldn't be. Everybody around here tilts a few back at some point or other. And if you don't kill yourself on Highway 231 or beat your wife then nobody sees much wrong in it, which they're not going to admit on Sunday morning, I can tell you.

"I guess ya'll got a limo then, huh?"

"Yeah, Brett's treat," she says, and squeezes his arm tighter.

Brett chimes in. "I like to help people out." What he means is he likes to shove his daddy's money in people's faces.

"Plus, we couldn't have any real fun worrying about driving. I only got two hands." He laughs like I'm supposed to give him a fist pound or something. I turn my head to throw a look at Thad, but he has pretty damn slyly slipped away. He hates Brett almost as much as I do.

"You know, Wee Wee . . ." Brett exaggerates his look down at me. "Man, you haven't changed a bit." This is Brett's way of saying, "You're still a sawed-off little punk."

"Yeah, well, some of us are just lucky, I guess." It's the only thing I can think to say.

"I'm glad Mandy invited me. This place reminds me of a lot of good times." He smirks at me. "You know what I mean?"

Every time I've seen Brett since his parents moved up to a huge place on Lake Martin in ninth grade, he hasn't failed to make a reference to when he yanked my pants down in the middle of PE. He got suspended for a day, and I got a nickname.

His words press down on me, crushing my insides until I feel just like I did standing in the gym with my gray shorts and white underwear lying on the floor.

This whole exchange makes me queasy. Mandy Pearman rejects me to go out with this. I'm so much better than this dickhead.

"Ya'll have a good time tonight." I walk away fast, heading to the one place I didn't want to go. But right now, the refuge is worth the price.

Samantha and Steven are excited to see me on the dance floor. The three of us dance (well, I do my best version of dancing) to a couple of songs until I can feel sweat starting to run down my back. The hip-hop sounds fade into a silence long enough to make the entire crowd look to the front to see what's going on.

Mr. Edwards' voice speaks into a mike at the d.j. stand. "Students, I hope everyone is having a good time tonight." He pauses for mocking applause. "But as all of you know, we're missing a special young man this evening—Mr. Paul Trahan."

The commons area falls dead silent.

"So we have something unusual for you. If I could have Mandy Pearman come up, please." Mandy walks up next to Mr. Edwards, and I wonder if he smells the liquor on her, and if he does, is he going to ruin this little moment? Not a chance. "We can all thank this young lady, Indians in Action, and the help of Ms. Hallman, our media specialist, for this treat."

Mr. Edwards nods a cue to Ms. Hallman. She wheels out a projector and a laptop mounted on a cart while a big screen like the one in front of the sanctuary at church comes down from the ceiling.

Ms. Hallman flips open the laptop, switches on the projector, and hits a few buttons. The crowd waits, barely moving. It takes about thirty seconds for the image to come up on the screen. But when it does, we're all staring at DJ, waving a wrapped and wounded arm at the web cam from his hospital bed. Everybody cheers and claps.

His face is still slightly swollen, but it beams anyway. He points at his right arm to show several of the *S O S* bracelets the IIA club has been selling. It's almost like our own Coosa Creek High School reality show.

The applause finally dies enough for Mr. Edwards to speak. "Paul, can you hear me?"

"Yes, sir." His voice comes from the d.j. speakers. Perfect.

"Can you see everybody here?"

Ms. Hallman steps out of the way so the web cam mounted on top of the laptop can show the crowd behind her.

"Kind of. It's dark."

Some of the students rush up close to the camera and start waving. DJ waves back, looking happier than a coyote in a chicken coop.

"Well, we all wanted to let you know how much we wish you were here with us, but we know you'll be back soon. We're all really proud of you."

A sting of jealousy shoots through me. I'm the one who saved him, after all.

"We're going to keep this party going, so sit back and enjoy," Mr. Edwards says in a way that only principals can. He hands the mike to the d.j. and the music comes back up. Almost everybody in the room hits the dance floor—definitely a record for an event at CCH.

On the screen, DJ does his best to move with the beat, which amounts to bobbing and bouncing his head. This is a great moment for him, but I can't help but feel a bit cheated.

Brett Toler takes Mandy's hand and spins her around. They dance so close I figure the friction will set Mandy's dress on fire, which might not be a bad thing. Maybe people aren't going to be different until you give them the chance. And that can start with a spark.

SIXTEEN

When Daddy cleanses people's souls in the big baptismal font that's more like a hot tub, he always recites the same scripture, then says, "I do this in the name of the Father, the Son, and the Holy Ghost." The Trinity. Kind of like oxygen, heat, and fuel.

The church's rooms and halls are empty. Steven fills the sanctuary with organ music so loud it nearly peels the paint off the walls. Daddy's holed up in his office making last minute "inspirational" changes to his sermon like he does every Sunday morning. And me and Thad are supposed to be finishing copying and folding today's bulletins.

He's at home, I'm sure nursing a throbbing brain,

and I'm staring at the church's fuse box trying to find the switch for the four and five year olds' classroom. Whoever wrote the labels must have been blind and crazy both. I can hardly read them. Beside the fact there's about a hundred of them. I run my finger up and down the rows of numbers written on the door of the fuse box until I find the number that looks somewhat like the right one. I flip it off.

My Sunday shoes echo down the hall, mixing with the beautiful stuff coming out the ends of Steven's fingers. I wish I could tell him what I'm doing. I think he'd almost understand. He knows like I do that doing the right thing sometimes doesn't look like the right thing at first.

I hit the light switch in the classroom. Nothing. Glad I got it right on the first try. Don't have time to run up and down the hallway all morning.

One of the things Mr. Simmons tried so hard to show all of us in his physics class was the practical, everyday application of physics. He doesn't want us just to know something, he wants us to be able to do something. So after our unit on electricity, he showed us all how to wire a wall outlet. And then showed us what could happen when it's not done right. He'd probably be glad I'm doing something with all that.

Only taking out four screws gets me to the wires. I quickly make the cuts and reconnections like I saw Mr. Simmons do in class. Then I take the plastic bag out of my pocket. I don't want to leave much to chance so I brought a bunch of cotton balls dipped in rubbing alcohol. I stuff them around the connections.

This is going to go fast. Nobody will get hurt. I'll make sure of that. The room and some of the hallway will get messed up, but these rooms are old, with wood paneling instead of drywall. Time for a change, anyway. And there are enough carpenters and electricians in the congregation who will do the repair work for free. Folks here like to win points with the congregation.

I screw everything back into place and repeat the steps on the outlet on the other side of the door. Just hope both sides go at about the same time.

You make the winds your messengers, fire and flame your ministers. —Psalm 104:4.

The early flow of people, those who show up for Sunday school, starts hitting the parking lot at 9:15. The bulletins are finished and set out at each entrance. I bounce back and forth from the entrances at opposite ends of the classroom hall, greeting folks, telling kids to stop running, and periodically checking for Mandy's car. It occurs to me that maybe she won't show up for the same reason Thad is MIA. I mean, Saturday nights have been known to make some Sunday mornings not quite so easy. But just as I check the time on the hall clock, she comes in the door looking like she had too much of a good time last night.

"Almost didn't expect to see you this morning. I was about to go find somebody to cover your kiddies."

She takes off her sunglasses. "Don't I wish. Mama drug

me out of bed this morning. If I would have stayed, she would have never let me go out with Brett again." She takes a mirror out of her purse to check her makeup and hair, not that the four and five year olds would notice. They love her.

"Well, can't say that's a bad idea."

"Oh, Wee Wee," she says with that get-over-it tone.

I watch her walk down the hall toward the classroom that's already filled with kids wound up like a sack full of monkeys. She goes in and shuts the door. About fifteen seconds later, just like I pulled a string, Mandy jerks the door back open.

"Wee Wee, something's wrong with the lights."

"The other classrooms seem to be fine. You want me to check the bulbs?"

She huffs. "Nah, don't worry about it. I'll open the blinds. That will be enough light for the little devils."

"Well, just to be sure, I'll check the fuse box."

"All right. Thanks." She shuts the door.

In front of the fuse box, the excitement stirring in my stomach makes me stop and soak up the moment, the anticipation. My heart pounds like I'm about to soar off a cliff.

One finger. One switch. One flip.

Snap.

I listen.

This shouldn't take long. The classrooms don't have a

sprinkler system like the sanctuary, but every room has a smoke alarm.

The second hand on the hall clock tiptoes past the numbers. Sweat sprouts on my forehead. Waiting is the worst, like Christmas. My heart thuds, my tongue's suddenly dry and thick. What if it's not working? If I did something wrong? No, I did it right. I had to. This is too important.

And then BEEEEEEEEEEEEEPPPPP! Mandy and the kids scream. People flood the hallway. I run, knocking some of them out of the way.

"Away from the door. Get back!" I yell. I turn the knob and kick the door open with my foot, not knowing how many flames wait on the other side.

When the door flies open, fire crosses the threshold like prison bars. A thick black smoke fills the top half of the room. Mandy and the kids huddle close to the window, frozen, petrified.

"I'm coming around," I yell. "And somebody call the fire department."

I nearly take the door off the hinges running out of the building to get around to the window.

"Mandy, break the window with a chair." Daddy had every window in the building nailed shut after the church got broken into and vandalized a couple times. "THE CHAIR. PICK UP THE CHAIR." But Mandy doesn't move. The kids scream. Her arms and body try to block them from the flames.

Wasn't planning on this. But I take off my shirt and wrap it around my fist and forearm. "DON'T LOOK." I rare back and smash the window like it's Brett Toler's face. Glass flies into the room. I keep smacking the glass until the whole bottom half is gone.

Black smoke billows into my face. "GET DOWN ON THE FLOOR. LOW AS YOU CAN."

When I climb through the window, they're a giant ball of shaking bodies. "All right," I say in the most casual voice I can muster, "let's get you all out of here."

The fire has grown to the ceiling. The smoke is thick like cloth. White powder covers the floor where somebody used the fire extinguisher. But they couldn't get to the flames from the hallway. Thank God nobody messed this up for me. For Mandy.

Somebody yells, "They're on their way. They're on their way."

My pager on my belt goes off. The truck should get here in time to save the other classrooms. I get to save what's important.

I snatch up the closest kid to me. It's balled up so tight, I can't tell if it's a little girl or boy. Billy Parker, the only fireman that shows up for Sunday school, stands outside the window with about ten other men.

"HERE." I hand the balled-up kid out the window.

"Keep 'em coming," Billy hollers back in the window.

"Mandy, get them lined up, just get them lined up to me."

She picks up her head, like, "What? Are you talking to me?"

"Come on now. Fast."

She looks over her shoulder at the fire that's swelling across the room and shakes her head. "They'll get burned."

"We're all going to burn up if you don't get going."

Mandy stares at me with the same eyes DJ had when he was laying on that grass—helpless, confused, wondering how things get away so fast.

"Look, you got to do this. Let's go. Come on, you can do it."

I step over, grab her under the armpits, and lift her up to her feet. She turns, stares straight into my face. "You see me now?" I say.

She nods.

"Then get those kids lined up."

Like a field worker tossing watermelons onto the back of a truck, I get every tot out the window in under a minute. But the smoke has really gotten to Mandy. She's on her hands and knees, coughing and wheezing.

"All right, Mandy, your turn." I put my hands around her stomach to help her up. My bare back feels like I'm laying on a bed of nails. "Might want to get moving before I'm a roasted marshmallow."

This isn't funny, but I want her to see I got it all under control, I'm not scared one bit.

She catches enough air to get up off the floor. I take her hand and walk her over to the window. "Now watch the glass." She's coughing too much to say anything. "You know I wouldn't let anything happen to you." She nods and pokes her head through the window far enough for someone to help her out.

The classroom is almost completely filled with fire. I wish I could stay for a while. I'm not afraid. I almost want to grab the flames and hold them in my hand. Chief said you can't catch it, but I'm not sure about that.

SEVENTEEN

By the time Chief Griffin shows up at the house to talk to Daddy, the dining room table is covered with enough food you'd think somebody died instead of lived. No real bodily damage done: Mandy ended up with a condition equivalent to smoking a pack of cigarettes all at once, and I would be worse off if I spent the day at the lake without sunscreen. But I guess Southern folks only know one way to show their concern and respect—with beef stew, green bean casseroles, and peanut butter brownies.

Daddy's tired and Mom's been shaking from either the thought of what happened or the hours between drinks, but they've been standing right there next to each other with me thanking people for their kindness.

"Brother Tucker, that's some boy you have there."

"He's just a Godsend."

"Thank the Lord for young men like you, William."

They all sang some version of praise while I stood there on the verge of embarrassment. I just don't take compliments as easily as Steven and Daddy. Could be because they're used to it, and I feel like I stole something.

Mom accepted the dishes and a few hugs from people she knew well but hadn't seen in a while. She even smiled and let Daddy put his arm around her shoulders. It struck me how long it's been since I've seen them touch each other for any reason. And even though Steven fielded phone calls in the kitchen the whole time, I'd say we looked like a happy family for the evening. Just not as happy as Mrs. Pearman.

I'm not sure what the record is for the number of kisses to a person's face without ever touching their lips, but Mrs. Pearman definitely gave it a go. She grabbed the back of my head with both hands and kissed my head, forehead, cheeks, nose, chin, and I shit you not, my eyelids. And then repeated about ten times, "My God, Wee Wee, what would we do without you?"

I wanted to wipe off the spit and lipstick covering my face, but no way was I going to do that right in front of her. I didn't know what to say, so Mom said if for me.

"Well, Sarah, you're going to kiss the boy to death."

"Oh, look at you," she said, and tried to wipe the traces of lipstick away with her thumb. "Mandy would have delivered those herself, but she's feeling a bit freaked out at the moment."

"I think we all are," Mom said while I wallowed in a momentary fantasy.

"Yeah, that fire could have really spread, maybe all the way to the sanctuary," Daddy followed up, drawing attention to what's really important. Even so, it was a nice time, if just for an evening.

Now the Chief wants to talk to both me and Daddy.

"I hate to barge in this time of night, but I like to do this while pictures are still fresh in everybody's head," he said when Daddy let him in the front door.

Both Mom and Steven retreat to their bedrooms. Daddy suggests sitting at the kitchen table.

"That'll be fine."

Chief Griffin takes out a spiral notepad and flips it open. "All right, I'll try to make this as quick as I can. I know you folks have had quite a day and you're ready to get to bed."

"What exactly can we help you with?" Daddy asks.

"Well, first, let me ask you: you know the last time the building's electrical system has been inspected?"

"Couldn't say. Don't know if ever, at least not since I've been pastor."

Chief Griffin nods. "The reason I ask is because electrical fires like that only start because somebody screwed up somewhere or a bolt of lightning came out of the sky."

"That part of the building is pretty old, though," I throw in.

"Yeah, William, it is, but not that old. What would you say, Brother Tucker? 1975?"

"That sounds about right."

Chief Griffin jots that down. He flips some pages back and forth. I realize I'm rubbing my palms so I put my hands in my lap. Chief stops turning pages and just stares down at his notepad. He shakes his head a little and then looks up at Daddy.

"Now for the not-so-pleasant stuff—not that anything about this is pleasant." He sets his pen on the table. "Brother Tucker, some of this might seem personal, so if you want William here to leave the room ... "

"Lord, Henry, I think William has earned his place at the table, so to speak." Daddy pats my shoulder. I know pride is a deadly sin, but man, it feels good.

"All right then." The Chief turns back a page in his notepad. "I had to write these down. My old brain ain't getting any better. About how many members have left the congregation in the past year?"

"Let me see. Not really sure. Maybe a dozen. I'd have to check the membership roster."

"And what were the reasons these congregants left?"

Daddy shifts in his chair. He's obviously uncomfortable with the question. Probably because Chief Griffin kind of makes it sound like Daddy did something wrong.

"You'd have to ask them."

"So you don't know of any of them having a problem with you or the church in general?"

"Henry, I thought you wanted to talk about the fire. What's this got to do with anything?"

Chief Griffin reaches in his jacket pocket. He pulls out a plastic bag half filled with charred bits. Some still have traces of white. Can't believe some of it survived. My ears start burning.

He leans across the table and opens the bag. "Take of whiff."

Daddy smells the contents. "Okay?"

"Smell like something familiar?"

"Ashes. That's about it."

"William?" Chief holds the bag for me to smell.

I can't play dumb. He knows better. During my training, he played this game where I had to identify different accelerants based on smell—gasoline, kerosene, rum, camp stove fuel, even cheap cologne and, of course, rubbing alcohol. I got them all right but one.

"Kind of like rubbing alcohol."

"Bingo." He looks over at Daddy. "Found this at the fire's origin. Know what that means, Brother Tucker?"

"You're saying somebody set the fire?"

"Exactly. And I can tell you, for somebody to set fire to a church, it would have to be awfully personal."

Daddy stares down at the table, eyes darting back and forth trying to find some reason in all this.

"So you can see why I'm asking."

Daddy nods.

"And I hate to say this in front of William, but I'm going to have to. Folks usually only get that mad when it has to do with either money or somebody's wife."

"Now just hang on a minute. If you're accusing me of what I think you are—"

"Look, I know you don't like it—"

"Oh no, I don't mind somebody coming in my house and accusing me of being a thief or a fornicator." Daddy's pissed. He always switches to sarcasm when he's ready to explode.

"But we ain't going to find who did this by walking around the truth."

"Well, there's not a shred of truth in what you're suggesting."

"All right then, all right then." Chief Griffin rubs the back of his neck while he studies his notepad. He isn't having any fun doing this. "Let's just switch gears for a minute."

"Good idea," Daddy says.

Chief Griffin checks his notepad. "Who is responsible for unlocking all the classrooms in the morning?"

Daddy looks at me. "William takes care of it usually before he handles the bulletins. But when he can't, it would be one of the deacons."

"And how many deacons we got?"

"Ten."

"And they all have keys."

"They do. But you can't think one of them ... "

"Brother Tucker, I'm just saying what I see. Can you give me all their names?"

Daddy rattles off the names of the deacons.

"Speaking of seeing," Chief says when he's finished writing, "William, did you see anybody unusual around the church this morning? Even though I don't think so, this could have been random, just somebody wanting to get off by setting something on fire."

"Can't say that I did." As soon as I say it I realize I should have lied. "But I wasn't really paying much attention. Maybe somebody could have been around."

A bit of silence hovers over the table while the Chief looks over notes he's made.

"How's all this going to affect getting the insurance money for repairs?" Daddy asks.

"Well, I'm sure the insurance fellas are going to want to see the report. I'm going to have to tell the police so they can help with the investigation."

"Investigation?"

"Yes, sir. It's pretty clear a crime has been committed here."

"But it wasn't by me," Daddy says.

"And as soon as we make that clear, I'm sure you'll be getting a check."

Daddy rubs his face with both hands like he wants the skin to just come right off. "Lord help me."

Maybe I should feel bad for him. But I don't know of

anything worthwhile that don't cause at least a little pain. Or a lot.

"Look here, don't worry." Chief Griffin closes his notepad and looks at both of us. "I know you ain't responsible for this. But I still have to dig into it. Couldn't call myself the chief if I didn't."

"I understand," Daddy says. "How long is all this going to take?"

"Well, I guess I'll go until I figure it out or I'm satisfied that it can't be figured out. And that's a possibility."

With the knot in my stomach, I have to keep reminding myself there's going to be something good in this, something new and clean. There has to be.

Daddy walks Chief Griffin to the door. It's a short goodbye, and Daddy catches me in the hallway before I can get to my room.

"I just can't tell you how proud I am of you, son."

That may not seem like much, but coming from a man who's always expected his kids to do right, no matter what, it's like hitting all six numbers in the Georgia Lottery.

EIGHTEEN

I know I can't be everywhere at once, but my head just won't accept that fact.

"William, I don't need a babysitter."

"Nobody said anything like that. What? I can't just walk with my brother to class?"

"You could if your class was even remotely near mine. Come on. Nobody is going to do anything."

I'm not so sure, now that Steven's told me some guys left a couple of pretty intense voicemails on his cell phone. He shrugged them off. "It's all talk."

"All right, I'll make you a deal," I say. "Let me walk with

you to first period, and I won't bother you the rest of the day."

"You'll let me handle this? No playing big brother or Mr. Hero or anything?"

"Absolutely."

"William, you must think I don't know you or something." He turns down C hall. "Okay, first period only."

"I guarantee."

Steven speeds up. "Whatever."

"I'm serious. Out of your hair for the rest of the day."

"Just got to take care of everybody, don't you?" he mumbles.

I ignore the comment. "So, how's Buck doing with all this?"

"Not as good as I am. He got some text messages from an "unavailable" number."

"What'd they say?"

"Same kind of stuff I got except just the text version. Something about him playing with boys' bats and what they were going to do with a baseball bat. So today he's playing sick. I told him that was the worst thing he could do."

"Maybe, but don't give him hell about it."

Steven gives me this look like it's too late for that.

"Well, don't give him any more."

Steven laughs just as a group of guys walks by. One of them coughs "homo" as they go past us.

"Really?" Steven stops and turns. "That's all you got?

Very original." He might as well be talking to himself because none of them even look over their shoulders.

"Oh, and the games begin," I say.

"I can handle that all day, and then some."

"I just hope they're not getting warmed up." I tug his arm to get him moving again.

"Ah, whatever."

I'm late for first period—and then second and third too. Instead of looking after Steven, I scan the halls for Mandy. No luck, though. So I give up and actually make it to fourth period on time.

Fourth has to be the worst period of the day because usually the only thought in my head is, "I hope I don't fall over dead before I can get to lunch." This helps keep me awake while Ms. Ayers drones on until we're all nearly comatose.

Somebody knocks on the door. Ms. Ayers stops to take a breath long enough to go over and open it. And in comes one of the office aids toting a massive collection of balloons—all colors with a big silver one in the middle with #1 on it.

"Mr. Tucker," Ms. Ayers says, "somebody is really liking you today." She gives me this little what-have-you-been-up-to smirk. "I'll just keep these over here so everybody can still see the board."

But I couldn't care less about the notes on the board. My eyes are zoned in on the envelope the balloons are tied to. That pink rectangle makes it pure damn agony waiting for the bell to ring.

"So, who's the admirer?" Ms. Ayers asks when I take out the card.

You're the Best, Dipshit! Samantha

I have to chuckle, even if it's wrapped in slight disappointment. "Just a friend of mine," I say to Ms. Ayers.

"That looks like more than a friend to me," she says.

"Nah, nothing else. We'd probably kill each other otherwise."

"Well, make sure you return the favor. Good friends are sometimes hard to hang on to."

"Will do, Ms. Ayers."

I have to say I feel like a complete jackass walking to the cafeteria with the Macy's Thanksgiving Day Parade–sized bundle trailing behind me. Only a blind person wouldn't notice. Most just smile at me and say stuff like "Wow" and "Whoa." But some say, "Happy Birthday," and "Congratulations." They're clueless.

Samantha's face nearly splits in half, she's grinning so big when I walk up to the table. "What do you think? Crazy, huh?" she says.

"Yep, I think crazy is the perfect word for you."

"I meant the size of that thing, but I guess crazy works for both."

I sit down. "You mind explaining this exercise in embarrassment?"

"Are you embarrassed? Sorry, not my intention at all."

"Which was…"

Her grin diminishes by half. "I saw your face the other night at the dance. You know, during the applause. Like I said, faces don't lie. I figured that since you're all the time doing things for others, somebody should do something for you."

"Samantha, I've just been doing my job. You wouldn't buy balloons for a farmer just because he grows good tomatoes."

"I guess. Still doesn't change the look on your face, though."

"I don't know what you're talking about."

"Come on, Will. Don't even try it. You were jealous. Maybe not green with it, but enough."

"Ridiculous. On your way home today, run by the doctor and get your eyes checked."

"Okay, Will, I'm not going to argue."

"That'll be a first."

"Anyway, so you were surprised, though, right?"

"Definitely. For a second I thought they might have been from Mandy. You know, from yesterday."

"You really have a thing for her, don't you?"

"Look at my face and you tell me."

Samantha stares like she's reading words written across my forehead. "Well, I think you'd be disappointed if she did go for you."

I pick up something in the tone of her voice. "Now who's jealous?"

"Anyway. Let's get out of here. Second part of the surprise."

"What?"

"Lunch. My treat. Come on." She gets up.

"You mean leave?"

"Uh, yeah. What? You want to hang around just so you can do physics problems out of the book? Can't wait for Mr. Simmons to get back? Plus, not like I'm eating *this* stuff." She starts to walk away. "Will, you know it's easier to leave if you actually stand up."

"Are you kidding? I'm a parade float with this thing. Not very inconspicuous."

"Leave them."

"But I don't want to." I feel like a six-year-old admitting it. "And I don't want to get suspended. On top of that, I have to take Steven home."

"Uhg, you're making this so much harder than it has to be. All right, give the balloons to me. I'll tell the office I'm putting them in my car so they don't get popped. Steven can drive, right?"

"Yeah."

"Well, get one of the office aids to take Steven your key. Satisfied?"

"But..."

"You know, for someone who puts out fires and saves people and shit, you sure are a scaredy cat."

The balloons fill the whole back of Samantha's car. "My God, I can't even see to back up." She swats a balloon out of her face. "What a couple of clowns." She laughs and puts the car in reverse. Her laugh disappears like she punched a button. All serious, she says, "Let us pray," before she hits the gas.

"Where are we going anyway?"

"Only the best for you, Will. The Waffle Hut."

The Waffle Hut used to be a Pizza Hut before the owners shut it down to build a new one out by the Walmart.

"High class."

"Going to be quite an experience." Samantha whacks the balloons back again. "If we make it."

There's a table open in the corner so me and Samantha slide in and grab menus. Rachel Rhodes, who used to go to school with us before she got pregnant, comes over.

"So what are we having to drink today?" She smiles, even though she's a little out of breath from scorching back and forth across the restaurant keeping up with tables.

"Coke for me."

"Coffee," Samantha says.

Rachel is too busy to write it down or even notice that we should be at school. She bolts away without giving us a second glance.

"Coffee drinker, huh?"

"Yeah. I blame my dad. He used to give me half coffee and half milk on below-freezing mornings in Iowa. I'm hooked now. No milk or sugar."

"Well, there are worse things to be addicted to."

"I guess."

We both peruse the menus in silence. I knew what I wanted before I walked in, so I put the menu down on the table and fidget with the aluminum ashtray that hasn't been used, at least not today. A book of matches with the Waffle Hut logo on it lies in the middle of the ashtray, and I can't help but strike one. It feels nice to hold the lit match until the flame barely grazes my fingertips, and I blow it out.

Samantha looks around her menu. "I'm sure your mother taught you not to play with matches, young man."

"Nope," I say, and strike another one. By the time it burns down, Rachel comes back with our drinks so I blow out the match and shove the matchbook in my pocket. She sets them down on the table and stops for a few seconds. "So, Wee Wee, some reason you're not at school?"

"We just decided to take a temporary leave of absence," Samantha answers for me.

"Don't I know the feeling. But it's going okay over at the school?" She says it like she misses an old friend.

"Just fine."

"That's good. I went ahead and got my GED before Chase was born, so I'm all done."

"That must be nice."

"Yeah." Rachel drops her eyes and grabs her order pad. "I guess that's what I get." She looks back at me and forces a smile.

I don't know what to say to that.

"So, ya'll ready to order?"

I turn my head back to the menu. "Looks like that patty melt plate is calling my name."

Rachel jots it down. "And for you?"

Samantha stares at the menu, still trying to decide.

"I love your shirt, by the way," Rachel says.

Samantha smiles bigger than I've ever seen. "Thank you." She looks back down and says, "I'll have two eggs over medium with toast and bacon."

"Grits or hash browns?"

"I'm in Alabama so I better have the grits. Wouldn't want people thinking I'm a Yankee or anything."

Rachel takes the menus, raises her eyebrows, and says, "I hear you, honey."

We pick up our drinks and take sips.

"Not a straw person, I see," Samantha says to me.

"Not since I was a kid. My parents would take us here on Friday nights, when it was a Pizza Hut, and the straws just made it so we would knock over our drinks. So Mom put an end to the straws."

I take another sip of Coke. As I'm mid-swallow, Samantha says, "So, how are your parents handling the whole our-son-is-gay thing?"

I choke down the mouthful of liquid, trying to look like the question doesn't bother me. "They're not."

"Steven's told them, right?"

"Nope. But I think they know anyway. Well, at least they've probably heard. Impossible that they haven't."

Samantha nods and takes a sip of coffee. "So how do you think they'll take it?"

This is so weird to be talking about, but it's also kind of a relief. "Hard to say. I mean, my dad is a minister, so he'll probably freak out and start quoting Leviticus. You know, 'abomination' and all that."

Samantha nods like she knows exactly what I'm talking about. "My dad's sister is gay."

She seems almost proud of it, so I tell her that.

"I guess I kind of am," she agrees. "Like I'm proud of Steven. It takes guts. I like guts."

"Really? I never would have figured."

My sarcasm makes her give me the finger while she takes a gulp of coffee.

"Your grandparents are okay with it?" I ask.

"Well, they're farmers in Iowa whose only son married a black lady, and their daughter is a lesbian and gay rights advocate. The holidays are a blast, let me tell you."

I have to laugh.

"Yeah, definitely not the crop my grandparents thought they were raising."

"I bet."

"My mom says it was pretty bad at first, but they eventually got over it. Just like your parents will." She seems so casual and sure about it.

"It's not really my parents I'm worried about." I look out the window. "Some of those guys at school scare me. They've always messed with Steven some when they weren't sure, but now that they are, they probably see it as a green light."

I keep looking out the window watching cars go by and start to worry about leaving school. At least Rachel brings our plates to distract me.

"Here you go." She sets down the plates. "Anything else right now?"

"No, Rachel, this looks fine."

"Well, ya'll just holler if you need anything."

I pick up half the sandwich to take a bite when I hear the door open. Leroy Toupes comes staggering into the restaurant.

He moves from table to table with his hand out, no doubt telling everyone it's his birthday. No one reaches back or goes for their wallets. They just shake their heads without looking up at him, and he moves on to the next table. One guy even slaps Leroy's hand away.

When this happens, the manager yells, "You old coot, get out of here."

Samantha drops her fork on the table. "I'll be right back."

She walks across the restaurant, and as the heels of her ropers bang against the floor, she tells the manager Leroy is with us. He holds up both hands. "Suit yourself. Just keep him under control."

That's almost funny. One thing I'm quite aware of is controlling a drunk is a near impossibility.

Samantha comes up behind Leroy, puts her hand on

his shoulder, and turns him around. She says something I can't hear and then hooks her arm around his elbow to lead him over. Nobody even glances up at them. They're probably just glad someone is getting Leroy out of their way.

When the two of them get back to the table, Samantha motions for Leroy to sit down first, then she gets in next to him. She pushes her plate in front of him and says, "Here, Happy Birthday."

"I remember you, pretty lady."

I'm surprised Leroy can even remember his name.

"Yeah, that's right." She pushes the plate a little closer to him. "Go ahead."

He picks up the fork, but pauses. He glances around the restaurant like this is some trick he's been roped into. He takes one bite and looks at Samantha. She smiles. "So how is it?"

He just nods with his mouth full.

You'd expect a homeless alcoholic like Leroy to carry a fairly dense cloud of stench with him, but the smell that blankets the table is surprisingly refreshing. As Leroy attacks the plate, I struggle to put my finger on it. He's halfway finished with the eggs and bacon before it hits me—mouthwash. He reeks of it.

We don't say a word the whole time Leroy eats. I don't even touch my patty melt because I can hear my dad quoting from the pulpit: "'I was hungry and you gave me meat; I was thirsty and you gave me drink; I was a stranger and you took me in; naked and you clothed me.'" So when

Leroy finishes Samantha's plate in record time, I slide mine over to him. "Don't slow down now."

Rachel even comes over and brings Leroy a glass of water. "Thought you might need this."

Leroy doesn't even look up so I tell her thank you.

Some people have left by the time Leroy finishes my plate. He picks up a napkin, wipes his mouth, and takes a deep breath and lets it out.

In his slightly slurred speech, Leroy says, "I think that there might have saved me. I almost feel human again." He says it like it's a joke, but I have to wonder how far from the truth it might actually be.

I raise my hand to signal Rachel to bring the check.

After dropping some cash on the table, leaving a pretty hefty tip, the three of us make our way to the parking lot. Samantha asks Leroy, "Do you need a ride anywhere?"

"No ma'am. I feel good enough to walk all the way to the Gulf of Mexico." He tucks his hands into the pockets of his ratty coat and heads for the highway. I hate to say I'm relieved.

"So, is Leroy your project or something?" I ask Samantha while we both watch Leroy walk up to the road.

"I don't know. Maybe. I just can't help it."

I know the feeling.

NINETEEN

Samantha gets me home in time to change for work, and Steven got my truck back unharmed. Can't say the same for him, though.

"Please tell me you got that at the batting cages." His left eye has a small cut. It's bruised and swollen.

"At least that's what Mom thinks," Steven says, picking through a pile of potato chips at the kitchen table.

I look behind me into the living room.

"She's taking a nap," he adds. "Dad's doing his usual, finding things to do at the church so he doesn't have to come here." It's a truth we rarely voice into the open air. When we're angry or resentful about anything in the universe, we tend to come back to the realities that grate our insides the most.

I pull out a chair and sit down. "So what happened?"

"Don't be stupid, Wee Wee. What does it look like?" Steven never uses my nickname unless I've done something wrong.

"Sorry, I mean, who?"

"Doug Sullivan."

"Just him?"

"Fortunately."

"So ... ?"

"So he's a dickhead. Jesus, I really don't want to give the play-by-play. My head feels like somebody is sitting on it."

"Man, I'm sorry."

"Stop saying you're sorry unless you want one of these to match," he says, pointing to his eye. "And where were you, by the way?"

"With Samantha. We went to the Waffle Hut."

"You're skipping class now? Mr. Hero can just do what he wants when he wants?"

"My bad." I know he's not really mad at me so I let him give it to me. This is what brothers do.

"Yeah, well, nothing you could have done. I didn't even see it coming. Barely even saw who it was."

"So, what? He just walked up and punched you?"

"I guess it doesn't matter I said I don't want to talk about it, huh?"

"You're my brother."

"All right, look, I was putting my stuff in my locker after school. I'm standing there tossing books in and BAM, the locker door slams into the side of my face. After my brain took a trip around a constellation or two, I focused enough to see Doug Sullivan walking backwards down the hall, laughing. 'Watch out there, faggot,' he said."

"And of course, you didn't tell anybody."

"Wouldn't have made my eye feel any better. Plus, I can't be some punk who runs and tells the teacher. That'll just make it worse."

"Maybe." I get up from the table. "So what now?"

"Nothing. Keep doing what I always do. I'm not hiding. Done enough of that." He finally picks up a chip and pops it in his mouth.

"Well, I got to get to work. Put some ice on that."

"Yes, ma'am."

———

I never thought I could feel such affection for cans of Chef Boyardee, but I'm loving these things. I lose my head in stacking cans like a robot—pick up, turn, place, pick up, turn, place. Almost downright hypnotic. The wall of red and green labels block every thought except how cool the Chef's hat is. Hey, anything is better than *Why haven't I heard from Mandy? Am I going to get suspended for skipping class? What is going to happen to Mr. Simmons? Would I feel guilty if I ran over Doug Sullivan with my truck?* If I let them, these questions that simmer somewhere down in the core of me are going to turn to a boil and cook me alive.

When I finish the ravioli I spend a half hour with the Jolly Green Giant, another fifteen with Mr. Peanut, and I know I'm losing it when I start talking to Mrs. Butterworth. She's quite a good listener, which is what I'm telling the bottles of syrup when Mandy Pearman comes out of nowhere.

"You know, somebody might think you're nuts." Her hair is up in a ponytail, no makeup, jeans and a T-shirt. I don't remember her looking better.

"Uh, well, right now, they wouldn't be far off the mark."

She smiles—a real one that our faces only produce when our heads won't give us a choice. "How are you? I mean, besides the talking to bottles of syrup."

"Right as the rain. But I should be asking you. You didn't come to school today."

"Nah." Her face changes. "Really didn't sleep much so Mama let me stay home."

"That's understandable."

"But I had to get out of the house. The walls were kind of closing in so she let me run down here for milk and coffee."

"You're okay and all?"

Mandy nods. "I'd be better if I could sleep."

Every time somebody tells me they didn't sleep well, it always feels like an invitation to pry, but that's not my style or my business. "Yeah, some sleep can cure a lot."

"Every time I close my eyes I can't not think about it." She stops and shakes her head a couple times. "And you."

"Me?"

"Yeah, like what if you hadn't been there? And then that got me thinking about how long I've known you, then how much I really don't."

"Oh, get out of here. You know me just fine."

"Apparently not. You know, some people say you see who a person really is when they're either drunk or under pressure."

"That's funny, because every time Thad drinks too much he has to hug me like a thousand times." I try to make the conversation lighter, but Mandy doesn't take the bait.

"Well, you weren't afraid at all. I saw you. All last night I went over and over it in my head. I was freaking paralyzed and you just acted like it was nothing. Where does that come from?"

I shrug one shoulder. "I don't know. Faith maybe. Just knew everything would be fine. Something in me, I guess."

"Well, you need to tell me where I can get it." She stops for a second and looks away like she's not supposed to say any of this. "I want to not be afraid."

"Mandy, just about anybody would have been out of their head scared in that situation."

"I'm not talking about the fire, Wee Wee. I mean all the time."

This is way too heavy for D&G. Her living room sofa or the front porch would be a better setting, but I don't have much to say right now. I keep my mouth closed for fear of prodding her along, not that she needs the motivation.

"I'm scared every day. Not like I was yesterday, of course, but dumb stuff—my hair not looking right, my outfit not matching, somebody laughing at me, not making a good impression." Mandy talks fast, like she's sprung a leak.

Just like with DJ, it occurs to me right then that maybe I don't have a right to hear all this. It's the stuff that you got to earn. And not because you did them a favor, but because you've traded the kind of words that breed trust and a knowing silence. I've wanted Mandy to talk to me this way for as long as I can remember, but I almost feel like a thief for listening to this. I'm sure I would, if I hadn't already given her the only gift I had to offer.

"I really thought I was going to die. But you, you … " Mandy can't finish the sentence. She's on verge of tears, but she holds them back and takes a deep breath. "Well, I'm not going to worry about the stupid shit anymore."

"Don't worry, you don't have to," I say.

She kind of chuckles. "Thanks for the permission, Wee Wee."

"No, I just meant … "

"I'm messing with you."

"Oh, yeah, right."

"Come here." She steps closer, leans over, and wraps her arms around me. "Thank you."

"No need. Just doing what I do."

… that when he comes, he will baptize you with the Holy Ghost and fire.

TWENTY

Samantha pulls up behind my truck just as me and Steven get out. She rolls down the window.

"I think I might start calling you Yoda," she says.

Steven laughs. "He's got the body, but I'm not sure about the brains."

Samantha looks over at Steven. "Whoa, that's quite a mug you're wearing there. What happened?"

"Cut myself shaving," he says.

"With somebody's fist?"

"Something like that."

"Anyway," I jump in, "why exactly would you call me that?"

Samantha keeps staring at Steven, obviously more interested in what he has to say. But she can tell he's not up for it and looks back at me. "Well, your wise words have given me some ideas."

"Oh Lord."

"What?"

"For some reason, you and ideas could be a bad combination."

"Whatever."

"And what exactly did I say?"

"You asked me if Leroy was my project."

"And…"

"I decided he is, along with a couple of other ideas. I went home and thought about it. I don't really do anything except go to school. Yeah, I put some stickers on my car, but I really don't do shit. So I'm going to do something."

"Should I be scared?"

"I'll let you know."

I pull my backpack on my shoulder. "You do that. So, can we go into school now?"

"You can, but I've got some things I have to do."

"You're skipping?"

"I don't really look at it as skipping, Will."

"And what would you call it, then?"

"Prioritizing." Samantha puts the car in drive.

"Hey, you want some help?" Steven asks.

"Wait, what are you doing?" I look at him like he's lost his mind.

"What? You can skip and I can't?"

"No, it's just—well, I thought you said you weren't going to hide."

"Not hiding, just taking a break." Steven walks over to the passenger side of Samantha's car. "Plus, if I'm here, you'll waste the day worrying about me. At least one of us should live up to the family name."

He gets in before I can say anything else.

"We'll catch up with you later," Samantha says and drives off.

———

I was jealous watching Samantha and Steven drive away, but by third period that wish-I-was-going feeling was replaced by glad-I-didn't. It's the first day in quite a while I've been able to really concentrate on what's actually happening in class. I didn't realize how distracted I've become.

Mandy is back. She's easy to spot in the hall because she's wearing the exact same thing she wore last night. And she's walking by herself, something as rare as snow around here. I smile and wave at her as she passes. She waves back and says, "Each lunch with me today?"

"Yeah, sure," I say automatically, before thinking it might be a bit awkward going back to that table. But turns out she doesn't want to sit there either.

"So, where do you want to sit?" she asks as we both walk away from the cashier.

We could go over to the table where I sit with Samantha,

but that feels almost like betrayal. "I don't know, wherever you think."

"How about out there?" She points to the benches outside the cafeteria in the commons area.

"Suits me all right."

We make our way out to the benches and sit with the trays balancing on our knees. "How's it feel?" I ask, hoping she knows what I mean.

"Good, I guess."

"So why no sitting where you normally do?"

"I don't know, actually. Just didn't feel like it. And right now, I'm just not going to do anything I don't feel like doing."

"I'm not sure how much your teachers are going to like that approach."

"Not classwork, dummy. You know what I mean."

"Yeah, I do."

We eat in silence for a few minutes, but not that crappy silence when you feel like you're lost in unfamiliar territory. Most of my close contact with Mandy has always been spent with me trying to impress her, make her smile or laugh, or some lame-ass attempt to prove something to her. But I guess I've proven everything I need to. Really, how much further can I go beyond pulling her away from what she saw as her own end?

She finishes most of her lunch and sets the tray on the bench. "So, tell me about Steven," she says, like she has no idea who he is.

"What do you mean?"

"Well, he's obviously out now."

"Yeah, pretty much." It feels scary saying it out loud here at school, to her.

"I can't believe he and Buck just showed up like that."

"Makes two of us, but you know Steven. He doesn't do anything halfway."

"I guess that's true."

"So, what do you think about all that?" I ask, really wanting her perspective.

"I think your dad is going to completely lose his mind."

"You're probably right. He probably already knows anyway. But in our house we're pretty good at ignoring things we don't like."

I take one more bite and set the tray next to me.

"I think he's doing the right thing, though," Mandy says.

"You do?"

"I really do. I think holding in secrets like that has to make you miserable."

This the first time I've come close to understanding why Steven came out. I guess he's done enough of keeping others' secrets that he couldn't hold on to one that big of his own. "You might be right."

The air feels a bit too heavy for school lunch so I ask, "Is this the new look you're going to be sporting from now on?"

"Pretty nice, huh?"

"Yeah, the I-slept-in-my-clothes-look is way under-rated, if you ask me."

She laughs. "Well, I didn't sleep in this. It just happened to be on the floor when I got up so I was like, 'What the hell.'"

"You pull it off very well. Might even start a new trend."

"God, I hope not."

"I don't know. You did pretty good with the bracelets." I point to the orange rubber band on her wrist.

Mandy's face turns a bit sad. "I guess DJ and I have something in common now."

I nod, because what can I really say to that.

"Maybe I'll go see him later."

"I think that would be good."

TWENTY-ONE

Samantha isn't the only one with priorities today, which is why when my pager goes off while I'm at the D&G, I don't even think twice about telling Mr. Whitehead I have to go. It's only a car fire, but it's still fire. So much better to be close to flames than detergent and toilet paper.

I chase the sun that's barely below the trees and catch up to the brush-fire truck. The old Impala is engulfed by the time we get there. The EMTs beat us there and they're looking over the old black man who was apparently driving the car. I can't hear what he's saying but he's fighting and waving them off like he doesn't want to be touched.

I only throw on my coat and gloves because this is

more like putting out a campfire than anything else. The Chief and Billy Parker don't bother with either.

"Hey, now look here, Billy," Chief Griffin says when he gets out of the truck. "We got somebody to do our dirty work this evening."

"Looks that way," Billy says. "Go on and grab that hose, Wee Wee. You're in better shape than both of us put together anyway."

That's not even close to the truth, but he doesn't know I don't need the excuse.

"My pleasure." I snatch the hose off the back of the truck and pull the heavy line over in front of the car.

The smell of burning rubber and plastic makes it hard to breathe, not to mention the black smoke blowing in my face. I signal for water and the hose jerks a bit when I open the nozzle. I stand firm, spray the grill of the car, and put out the engine in a matter of seconds. The windows are down so it doesn't take long to extinguish the inside either. Only three minutes and the flames are gone, leaving nothing but a skeleton on the side of the road. It's a nice three minutes anyway.

Chief Griffin and Billy Parker see the grin stretched across my face. "You love this, don't you, son?" Chief says.

"I think that would be putting it mildly."

"Look at him, Billy. He's as giddy as a school girl."

I am. I can't tell you the feeling of control and presence that gushes inside me. I'd say it's almost spiritual.

"Better watch that," the Chief says. "That kind of attitude will get you in trouble."

"Yes, sir."

The Chief motions for me to get the hose back on the truck. "Billy, you got your phone on you? Call up Leonard and tell him to pick this thing up."

While I struggle to get the hose back in place, the EMTs finish fighting with the old man and leave him standing there in the grass.

"How's it coming back here?" The Chief walks over to check my work.

"It's a lot easier to get it off, let me tell you."

"That it is, that it is. You look like you're dancing with that thing."

"Whatever it takes, I guess."

I struggle a bit more and finally get the hose back up on the truck right. Billy has already climbed into the cab. I know he's in a hurry to get home and finish dinner, but I have to ask the Chief, "So, any progress with the fire at the church?"

"Naw, not really. I still know the fire was set, but fire-setters are hard to catch. A lot of the time they don't get caught unless they screw up. But tell your dad not to worry. We'll get his name cleared so he can get his insurance all situated."

"Will do, sir."

"Now go on home and throw them clothes in the trash.

You're mama won't ever get that burnt-rubber smell out." He slaps me on the shoulder and climbs in the truck.

The Chief gets the truck turned around and heads back to the station. I notice the old guy still standing over in the grass looking like "what the hell just happened?"

"You got somebody to come get you?"

"Not unless God himself drops down a couple of angels. And hell, if he's going to go through all that trouble, he might as well take me instead." He rubs the top of his head and sits down on the grass like he's content to sit right there and wait to see which one of those things will happen.

I pull off my jacket and gloves and put them in my toolbox. "Hey, come on. Can't let you sit here on the side of the road."

"Sonny, don't you worry about me. You go on ahead."

It's a good four miles to anything, and Daddy didn't raise me like that.

"I'm not going to be able to do that, so why don't you just climb in and let me get you home." I'm sure Samantha would offer him dinner too, but I figure a ride is good enough.

He sits there until he can get enough anger out of his way to get up and walk over to the truck. He's still got a scowl across his face when I unlock the door for him.

"Sorry about your car."

"Yeah, yeah."

"Hey, maybe you'll get something better."

My house feels like a crime scene when I come in. Lights are on, but there isn't a sound. Dishes of food, plates, and glasses still cover the kitchen table. Chairs are shoved back out of place. Tension and dread are nothing new to this house, but this is different. It's so damn eerie I'm almost afraid to disturb the air, like the boogieman will hear me and come get me too.

I can see across the living room that the door to Daddy's office is closed. I listen for the sound of the TV in my mom's room, but I can't make out anything. I would go check, but I'd rather stick to the safe side of the house where my and Steven's rooms are.

I tap on Steven's door. He doesn't answer, but I turn the knob anyway. He's sitting on the edge of his made bed staring straight at the wall.

"Steven, man, what happened? It feels like somebody died."

"I guess you could say that."

"What? Who?"

"Me."

"Huh?"

"They know." Steven doesn't look up, flinch, shrug, or anything.

"So you told them."

"Kind of had to. Somebody at the Bible study last night told him about me and Buck at the dance. He wouldn't say who, but a kid told their parents and they told him. Sort of my plan anyway, so I guess I should be glad."

"Looks like it didn't go too well. I saw the table just left like that."

"Be glad you missed it."

"At least it's out in the open. That's what you wanted, right?"

"Yeah. I guess I'd deluded myself into thinking maybe they wouldn't freak. Dad yelled. A lot. Mom was like you'd expect—nearly catatonic. I thought maybe she'd at least try to say *something*. Not that the pastor gave her much of a chance."

"So what now?"

"That's what I've been trying to figure out. I remember hearing 'not under my roof' and 'not in my church,' then somewhere in there, 'not my blood.' And I'm pretty sure the last word he said before storming off to his office to pray was 'burn.'"

Steven leans over and puts his face in his hands, not like he's sad, just kind of like he wishes he could relax.

"So, what? He wants you to leave?"

"I guess we'll find out." He looks up at me and smiles with only one side of his mouth, as if to say, "Sorry about the mess I made."

"Hey don't worry. He's just upset right now. He'll get over it."

Steven straightens his back and takes a deep breath like he just woke up. "You know, William, I don't care if he does or doesn't. This is it. This is who I am. *He* can deal with it any way he wants. I'm not going to feel bad about this."

"You shouldn't."

"Thanks, little brother."

"All right, well, I'm going to clean the kitchen."

"I'd offer to help, but you smell like death twisted around a lollipop." Steven waves the air away from his nose.

"Car fire. Don't worry. These are going in the trash."

I step from his doorway, but he calls me back. "Hey, by they way, wait till you see what me and Samantha are doing tomorrow morning." He beams like the entire episode earlier didn't even happen.

"I need to worry, don't I?"

"Depends on Mr. Edwards' position on matters of a sexual nature."

"Oh, shit. Come on. Out with it."

"Nope, you'll have to wait." He falls over on the bed and lies with his hands laced behind his head, gloating in the pleasure of keeping me out of the loop on this.

"That's fine. I can't fit another thing in my head right now, anyway."

"Not that you had much room to start with." He laughs with an ease that shouldn't be on a night like this. And I realize maybe I've been partly wrong about my brother. I've always thought Steven plays the organ at church because he likes being part of services that save folks as much as he likes the music and performance. I figured maybe he feels the same obligation that's gnawed at me my whole life, to uphold the Tucker name like a proud flag to be flown for the whole town to see.

But that's not so.

Daddy tells Steven and me the same thing every time one of us leaves the house: "Remember who you are." Now I know it meant something totally different to each of us. I knew I was Pastor Tucker's son and that meant I had to act a certain way. Steven, though, has been trying to figure out who he is for years. And he's getting closer every day, and he's definitely not somebody who feels like he's got to answer to anyone but himself. I don't know if I'm scared or envious.

I do my best to clean up the kitchen. I wash dishes, spray and clean counters. I even sweep so it looks like supper didn't even happen. And maybe tomorrow, we'll act like it too.

TWENTY-TWO

Samantha picked up Steven before I even got out of bed, or anyone else did for that matter. He just poked his head in my room and said they had to make some last-minute preparations. His comment definitely didn't make me any more excited about getting up and going to school.

Mom and Daddy stay tucked away while I leave. Maybe they don't want to see me either, perhaps pretend they don't have children for now. Not that I blame them.

I get out the door quite a bit earlier than normal, really by accident. Or maybe I can't seem to lose that urge to protect my brother from himself, even though he reminds me too often that I don't have to.

Steven isn't hard to spot when I pull into the nearly empty parking lot. He's wearing a helmet-looking thing with reddish bristles on top, reminiscent of an ancient Roman soldier. I'm baffled.

"Are we putting on a play this morning?"

"How do you like it? Samantha made it." He runs his hand back and forth across the bristles.

"Yeah, it should get some attention," Samantha says, and walks to the back of the car.

"Now can I know what you're doing?"

Samantha says "Okay" and grabs the handle to the hatchback. She looks at Steven, smiles, and then looks at me. "Ready?"

"No, but go ahead."

She pulls open the hatch to reveal four cardboard boxes filled with small brown paper bags, each one rolled down to the size of a fist with a rubber band wrapped around it. She acts like she just performed a magic trick. "Ta-Daa!"

"Okay. What the heck? What is all this?"

"CONDOMS!" she screams.

"Jesus, are you opening up a whorehouse or what? Samantha, this isn't Nevada."

"Yeah, no kidding."

"Where did you get so many?"

"The county health department. We spent just about the whole day putting them in the bags. You should have seen those ladies down there. They just thought this was the greatest idea."

"I used to think you were a little nuts, but now I'm sure of it. Both of you." I stare down at the boxes. "What do you plan to do with these?"

"And I used to think you were smart. Hand them out to everybody, of course."

"Oh, this will be just fantastic."

"Hey, did you know that HPV is the leading cause of cervical cancer, and teen pregnancy is the number one cause of teenage girls dropping out of high school? Just like Rachel at the Waffle Hut. That was when I got the idea."

Her comment makes me remember my daddy telling me one time that too much information can be a bad thing.

"And that doesn't even count AIDS, herpes, gonorrhea..."

Samantha shares the information she got at the health department a little too loud for me to be comfortable. "Okay, okay, you want to keep it down?"

She sees the look on my face and her excitement drains a bit. "You don't think it's a good idea? That students obviously need these?"

Samantha is right. I don't remember ever going to Coosa Creek without at least half a dozen girls handing out invitations to baby showers before graduation invitations were even ordered. And there was an article in the paper after last year's blood drive before prom that showed a pie chart indicating that of the 107 pints of blood collected, twenty-two couldn't be used because of STDs.

"I just think you might be asking for trouble, is all."

"There isn't meth in these bags."

"Yeah, but this is Alabama. This is just something folks don't want to have out in the open."

"That's not the only thing," Steven says.

"That's the problem, Will," Samantha says. "The town I used to live in was the same. People wanted to act like if they didn't talk about it, it didn't exist. And this might not be the solution, but I have to try."

I wipe my hand across my forehead and nod because I know, regardless of what I think, they're doing this.

Samantha grabs one of the cardboard boxes and tells Steven, "Hey, don't forget the sign."

He pulls out a piece of posterboard with *The best offense is a good defense* written on it. He sees my face. "I figure this would appeal to the football players. I mean, from the way they play most of the time, it's obvious they score more off the field than on."

"I really can't believe this."

"Hey, Will, grab a box," Samantha says.

"Oh, no. I'm not sticking my hand in any part of this."

"That's good, because they're not for your hand."

"So funny."

"Just grab a box, you big baby."

Steven puts his sign on top of a box and pulls it out. "Come on. Take you two seconds."

I almost sprint to the sidewalk in front of the school and drop the box. After Samantha drops hers, she goes back for the last one.

They get set up with their sign and Steven in his ridiculous hat and wait for people to show up. I can't stand here. "Well, I'm going to leave you to it." I shake my head at Steven. "I can't believe you're doing this."

"Now little brother, got to be prepared for the worst. Or I guess I should say the best." He laughs.

I eye the bench by the bus lane, where I can watch from a safe distance.

"Wait," Samantha says to stop me. "Take one."

"No thanks. I'm all for being prepared, but when you live in the desert, you don't have much need for a raincoat. You know what I mean?"

Steven unzips my backpack and shoves one of the little paper bags in anyway.

As students walk by, the two of them hand out the paper bags, only saying, "Here you go." Nobody really bothers to look inside immediately. They're more concerned with laughing at Steven's hat. It matches the bruise on his face pretty good. And of course no one refuses, because everybody likes free stuff.

When the buses arrive it gets really hectic, folks being driven, I'm sure, by curiosity at anything different at the beginning of a school day. A mob starts to form when Steven and Samantha can't keep up with the flow of traffic. But that mob disperses like somebody dropped a grenade when Mr. Edwards comes storming toward them like a bull.

Mr. Edwards blows right by me. "The two of you, just hold it right there," he says.

I join the train of folks heading into school. I don't want to hear any of this. Mr. Edwards has already got one of the boxes in his arms, and Samantha has her hands latched onto it, trying to pry it away. Steven grabs an armful of bags out of another box and starts just throwing them at people who back away. Mr. Edwards drops the box he's holding, scattering bags on the sidewalk, and grabs the radio clipped to his belt. This isn't good at all.

I step inside, at least content with the fact that I warned them.

Students have opened the bags to find the surprise inside. And just like I expected, there's lots of laughter and snickering. Some of the guys have already blown air into condoms and are batting them around like balloons at a birthday party. I'm sure Samantha would prefer they all take it more seriously, but what do you do.

Mr. Gholston and Mrs. Shook, our two other administrators, come scorching across the commons heading for the door, no doubt responding to Mr. Edwards' radio call. I step out of the way to let them out the front. I don't even think about the consequences Steven is going to get handed. He's just pouring gas on a fire.

The bell rings, and the mass of students respond like we've been trained and head to class. The blown-up condoms get a few more whacks, but people let the fun die down and accept that the day must go on like normal. Safer? Maybe. Happier? At least for the time being.

Mr. Edwards, Mr. Gholston, and Mrs. Shook come

through the doors with Samantha, Steven, and four empty boxes in tow. Samantha and Steven couldn't look more like they just won a race if they'd crossed the finish line in the Montgomery Marathon miles ahead of everyone. I've never been in trouble at school, but I can't think I'd enjoy it nearly as much as the two of them seem to be.

Samantha is talking steadily. "Aren't you tired of pregnant girls dropping out of school? How do you think they got that way? Ever heard of AIDS? We could have saved somebody's life today."

None of the administrators respond. They just keep their eyes straight ahead, dragging the two of them by the arm. When they walk past me, Mr. Edwards looks right at me and says, "I expect a whole lot more out of Pastor Tucker's boys."

I try to give him a look that says, "I didn't have anything to do with it." But I know it doesn't matter to him. I'm linked to Steven by blood, by last name. And to some people, that means our sins are shared as well.

The talk around the school is not what I expected. I figured there'd be jokes, but thought they'd be laced with bubble gum and Altoids, not acid and venom. By the end of the day, Samantha is a whore and I can't even bring myself to repeat the words I hear partnered with my brother's name.

A lot of these people could use a good fire.

TWENTY-THREE

Going home isn't an option I'm even going to consider. I almost want to go into work, even if this is one of my few days off. But that would probably mean answering questions or telling lies, neither of which I have the stomach for right now. I wish my pager would save me, give me a direction and purpose for the rest of the day.

Samantha does instead.

"Hey," she says on the other end of my cell phone, "so how did the day go?"

"Well, you're a whore now. At least that seems to be the general consensus around Coosa Creek High School."

She laughs. "Oh, that's great."

"Great?"

"Yeah," she says. "I mean to stir up people like that."

"Samantha, I really don't get you sometimes. Wait, what am I talking about? All of the time."

"That's fine, you don't have to."

"Good, since there's not much chance I ever will." I think that for someone who just got suspended, she sounds as happy as a pig in the mud.

"Hey, what are you doing right now?" she asks.

"Nothing. I don't have work and I sure don't want to go home. Can't imagine what I'll find. By the way, how pissed are your parents?"

"Not at all. They're behind me one hundred percent."

"Get out of here."

"Yeah. They're actually proud of me. But anyway, forget that. I need you to do me a favor."

"What's that?"

"Meet me downtown in an hour. At that old auto parts store. I need a chaperone. My mom's orders."

"For?"

"Safety. She doesn't want me to go by myself."

"I mean, for what?"

"Oh, right. To see Leroy. One of my new projects, remember? Don't worry. You'll like this."

"Yeah, I can do that. But you'll have to do something for me."

"Sure," she says.

"Don't you want to know what it is, first?"

"Not really. You need me? I'll do it."

Fall has finally fully arrived in Coosa Creek. The wind blows cool without the moisture that warmer months carry up from the Gulf of Mexico. It's always the first sign that things have shifted and we've made the turn toward winter. I stand next to my truck on Main Street, letting the breeze offer me a taste of relief to my ragged insides.

Samantha drives up and gets out with a cardboard box, like the ones that were filled with condoms this morning. But this one has food, a blanket, socks, underwear, some overused paperbacks, and a bag of candy.

"My Lord, when you get some ideas, you don't wait around, do you?"

"What's the point in waiting?"

I have no answer.

Samantha looks around. "He's not here?"

"Could be inside. It's getting dark—and cold."

Everybody in town knows Leroy sleeps in the abandoned auto parts store, but they do what they've always done. Ignore him. I guess they figure the store going out of business and Leroy Toupes are both better left forgotten.

"There's a way in?"

I shrug, like how am I supposed to know. "Must be."

Samantha takes off around the side of the building, and I follow like I'm hitched to a leash. Around the back there's an aluminum bay door that's bolted down to the concrete. Next to it is a metal door with the doorknob beaten off.

I step around Samantha and nudge the door open with my foot. I can't see a damn thing, but my nose is absolutely assaulted. The place is filled with a potpourri of mouthwash, urine, stale wine, and leftover fan belts and radiator hoses.

Once over the threshold, I yell, "Leroy? Mr. Toupes?" My voice echoes through the empty metal shelves and off the concrete floor. No answer.

Samantha walks up behind me and we both move a little farther into the building. I call Leroy's name again, and hear what sounds like a bottle spinning on the floor.

"Get out of my house." Leroy's angry voice is barely understandable.

"Mr. Toupes. We brought a few things," Samantha calls, as sweet as I've ever heard her.

"I'ma cutcha ifyadon't getouttamy house." The words run together, making him sound more Neanderthal than usual.

"Hey, maybe we should just let him be. Pissed off drunks aren't fun to deal with."

"Well, nobody promised this would be fun." Samantha goes around me and starts walking in the direction of Leroy's voice. I don't remind her she said I would like this.

"Wait, hang on. You don't know … " I stop because it's useless. Samantha isn't going to listen to a word I say.

"I said getouttahere or I'macutcha," Leroy yells again.

"We're just here to help, Mr. Toupes," Samantha says.

Leroy doesn't reply right away, but I can hear him moving, bottles clinking into each other.

"Don't need no help," he finally says, slower, clearer. He strikes a match and light fills up the far corner of the store.

Through the legs and platforms of empty shelves, I see Leroy lying on the floor. We step around the last row of shelves to stand about ten feet away from him.

He lays on a pile of cardboard with what looks like an old curtain covering up his legs. Empty mouthwash and wine bottles make a nest around his feet. An old oil lamp shines bright beside him, and he holds a metal object in his hand that looks like a homemade knife.

I put my hand in front of Samantha to keep her from walking any farther.

"Mr. Toupes, do you remember us? You ate with us at the Waffle Hut."

He looks at us for a second, trying to remember. I'm sure all the alcohol that's coursed through his veins the past forty-eight hours makes it hard to get ahold of any memory older than a few minutes. But the angry lines on his forehead finally soften. "Yeah, I do."

Samantha holds up the box. "I got some things I thought you might need—a small blanket, a pack of socks, some books in case you get bored." She sets the box down on the concrete floor. "I made a few sandwiches and put them in there too."

Leroy sits all the way up. "Sandwiches? What kind?"

"Turkey. I hope that's okay."

"Well, it ain't a hot plate, but they'll do." Leroy scoots over and looks in. "Now ya'll goandgetouttahere. You weren't invited. Can't just barge into a man's house like this."

"We're sorry, Mr. Toupes," I say.

"Yeah, is there anything else we can do for you?" Samantha follows up.

Leroy rummages around the empty bottles, obviously trying to find one with a couple swallows left in it. Then he grabs the box and pulls it closer and looks in. "You got everything in here but the mouthwash."

"Well, sir, I didn't think that would do much for you," Samantha says, knowing good and well he'd drink it.

Leroy snaps his head up at her. "What the hell do you know?"

I put my hand on Samantha's arm. "Come on, let's go." I know this is the point where it could get ugly.

"Yeah, goandgetouttahere. Nobody asked you to come in here. This is my house."

We take a few steps backward and then turn and walk away. I can hear Leroy tear into the pack of socks behind us.

When we get back out on Main Street, Samantha says, "That didn't go like I planned. I mean, when was the last time that man had a clean pair of underwear?"

"Well, like he said, he didn't ask for it."

"That shouldn't matter."

"No, it shouldn't. But to him it does."

"I don't get it."

"I guess maybe since he didn't ask for it, then you just reminded him he can't help himself."

"Well, whether he likes it or not, I'm going to keep doing it."

"I know you will."

She leans back against her car. "I wonder how long it's been since he's slept in a real bed." Her gaze is glued to the front of the building. "You know, I don't know if I could live like that."

"Yeah, that's pretty rough."

"But hey." She raises her hands in the air. "I'm going to do as much as one person can do."

I pat her back. "I think you'll be surprised at how much that actually is."

She nods and finally takes her eyes off the building. "So, you did something for me, now I get to do something for you. What'll it be?"

"Come to the school board meeting with me tonight."

TWENTY-FOUR

I've heard stories about lifeguards who go out to save a drowning swimmer, just to have the person fight them so bad the lifeguard has to let them go or risk drowning themselves. I wonder how they live with that, knowing they were that close to saving someone but couldn't do it.

The only students sitting in the audience at the school board meeting are me and Samantha. I'm surprised, or maybe I'd call it disgusted. The things that man has done, and they can't even be bothered. And Mr. Simmons notices.

He keeps turning around, scanning the crowd. I can see it right there in his eyes. He's looking for the people who really should be here shouting his praises.

He sits in the front row, and a few seats away, Mr. Edwards and Mr. Cronyer, the president of the PTA, wait for the board to reach that particular bit of "business."

The meeting starts with Mrs. Teschner. As soon as she gets up to the podium, she tears into a rant for about fifteen minutes about how the cafeteria menu is the reason her son is overweight. She whips out binders from a cardboard box and hands them to each board member, then proceeds to give the whole room a lesson in nutrition. Her final challenge is for each board member to eat in the school cafeteria every weekday for a month to see the impact it has on their health. I count six out of the nine bellies at the table already looking fairly round so I doubt she'll have any takers.

Next up is Ms. Deana Hartley, the cheerleading sponsor at Coosa Creek. She's here to appeal to the board for money to buy her squad mats. After reading her statement, she asks that the lights be turned down. Then she shows a PowerPoint with charts on how there are more injuries in cheerleading than in any other high school sport, and videos of girls busting heads, ankles, and wrists on basketball courts and tracks, and even some poor girl who got dropped during a pep rally and knocked slap unconscious. I almost feel sorry for Ms. Hartley, because some of the audience and even some board members snicker all the way through like this is an episode of *America's Funniest Videos*.

When the lights come back up, Ms. Hartley waves at somebody in the back of the room. We all hear the door open so the whole room turns. In walks a guy in a full Coosa Creek Indian football uniform, but I can't tell who it is under the helmet.

The anonymous football player stands next to Ms. Hartley while she writes prices on sticky notes and places them on each piece of equipment. Then she holds up a piece of posterboard to show the members the total amount spent on each uniform. The audience can't see the figure, but from some of the eyes jumping out of the heads of the folks at the table, it's got to be pretty ridiculous.

Mr. Dunn, the board chairman and owner of First Federal Savings and Loan, pipes up real quick. "Ms. Hartley, as I understand it, part of the costs for providing uniforms for the football team are offset by contributions by the team booster club." He smirks.

"No, sir." She pulls a piece of paper out from an envelope. "According to Rocky Gaudin, the booster club president, the majority of the funds raised by that organization go to providing team meals before games, letterman jackets and awards for players, and the team's banquet at the end of the season."

Mr. Dunn looks at Ms. Hartley like she just peed on his shoes. "I appreciate your preparation and passion on this matter, but unfortunately there is nothing we can do. The athletic budget for this year has already been set."

And he doesn't look like he's sorry one bit. I could have told Ms. Hartley she wasn't going to get too far with folks around here by criticizing the football program. This is Alabama.

She stands there for a few seconds like she's not ready to accept that explanation, so Mr. Dunn says, "Thank you, Ms. Hartley. That will be all."

Ms. Hartley looks downright heartbroken when she takes her seat, while some of the board members check their watches like they got somewhere to be. Not a drop of sympathy among them.

Mr. Cronyer is called up to begin the business concerning Mr. Simmons. Mr. Cronyer straightens his tie and buttons his suit coat as he approaches the podium. He places his leather binder down and flips it open, then starts to read a statement.

"The job of every school employee is to ensure a safe environment where our young people can receive a first-rate education. As parents in our community send their children to school, they have to be able to trust those who are charged with the care and oversight of those children. It's the least they can expect from the tax dollars they provide for the schools' operation." He stops and clears his throat.

"In this case, we have a veteran educator who, unfortunately, did not take the necessary precautions to ensure the safety of everyone involved in a science experiment, which I have to remind the board was not approved by the school's administration. Because of Mr. Jerry Simmons' lack of preparation, parent notification, and guidance by the school administration, one of his students nearly lost his life. If it wasn't for the brave action of another student, not the teacher, this boy certainly would have died. I think the board will agree with me that this type of recklessness cannot be tolerated if we're to provide the type of education our children deserve. Therefore, unfortunately, the PTA and myself believe it is in the best interest of the students that Mr. Simmons be terminated, replaced with a teacher with greater concern for safety. Thank you."

This guy makes it sound like Mr. Simmons didn't care what happened.

Mr. Edwards replaces Mr. Cronyer at the podium. But he doesn't have a prepared statement. He's here to field questions from the board.

One of the ladies on the board looks at some papers in front of her. "Mr. Edwards," she starts, "I see that Mr. Simmons has received what I would call stellar evaluations by you over the past ten years. Do you believe your evaluations of his performance are accurate?"

"Yes, ma'am, I do."

"I see here that you've used words like attentive, innovative, hands-on, energetic. Are these qualities you'd like to see in all of the teachers under your guidance?"

"Absolutely," Mr. Edwards says.

Thank God for this lady. I need to kiss her when this is over.

"Well, then, I have to ask you ... " She pauses. "Do you think the school would be better or worse off having Mr. Simmons on staff?"

I hold my breath.

"Ma'am, I'd have to say better."

She nods her head while I let out my breath.

"However," Mr. Edwards starts back up, "that does not necessarily outweigh Mr. Simmons' responsibility in this matter."

"So is it your intention here to place blame, rather than accept that this was an unfortunate accident during a well-prepared, inventive experiment?"

"Ma'am," Mr. Edwards begins, but the lady cuts him off.

"Do you place any responsibility on the shoulders of the injured student?"

This question invokes some murmurs and mumbles. Obviously the room isn't comfortable placing blame on DJ.

Mr. Edwards waits for the murmurs to dissipate. "I guess I could, if Mr. Simmons had notified the class and their parents of the type of experiment they were to be involved in and the type of clothing they should wear. But no such notification was given."

She nods again and then asks the other board members if they have further questions for Mr. Edwards. They don't, so Mr. Edwards sits, and Mr. Simmons stands up and faces the firing squad. His head is nearly hanging to his knees. He looks like a man who's beat himself up so much there's really nothing left for others.

He has no binders or PowerPoint, not even a sheet of paper. He just grabs the sides of the podium like I've seen

Daddy do during sermons when he wants to say something important.

"I've been a teacher for over twenty years. And during that time my goal has always been the same. I try to push my students academically and show them the practical and real-world applications of science. I'm not there to transfer knowledge from my brain to theirs. I've always hoped to help them make their own discoveries." He stops for a second because his voice quivers.

"But I know it's *my* classroom, *my* experiments, so ultimately I'm responsible for what happens. I agree with Mr. Cronyer that it's my job to ensure a safe environment."

I want to jump out of my seat and stop him.

"I did not give the proper notification to the students or their parents. I thought I had covered the necessary variables, but it's obvious to us all I had not. All I can say is that my intentions were good, and if the board allows me to continue teaching here in the community I love, I can promise such an oversight will never happen again. Thank you."

Mr. Dunn waits for Mr. Simmons to sit before he speaks. "The board will now vote on the matters set before us this evening."

I can't help it. I have to say something. I jump up out of my seat. "Excuse me. Can I just...?" I move toward the podium.

Mr. Dunn looks at me like he really doesn't want this. But I keep talking anyway.

"My name is William Tucker. I'm a senior at Coosa Creek. Mr. Simmons is my teacher."

Mr. Dunn gets out of his chair. "Son, I'm sorry, but we don't have time ... "

The lady that made Mr. Simmons sound good cuts him off. "Oh, I think we have a few minutes. Go ahead, Mr. Tucker."

Mr. Dunn sits back in his chair.

The podium reminds me how short I really am. I can barely see over the thing, which makes me feel out of place, inadequate maybe. I tilt the mike down before I say whatever the heck I can figure out to say to save Mr. Simmons' job and the rest of our year in physics.

"Besides being one of Mr. Simmons' students, I'm also a member of the Coosa Creek Volunteer Fire Department. I've received training that would allow me to perform as a firefighter just about anywhere."

Mr. Dunn jumps in. "Yes, son, we all know who you are. And thank you for what you did."

"Well, you should be thanking Mr. Simmons. He did everything he could do to make that experiment go well. He had two fire officials present, including me. He gave detailed instructions and precautions. And besides that, he's the best teacher any of us has. But accidents happen— in the real world—and that's what he's preparing us for. Heck, you don't try to fire the biology teacher if some kid drops a scalpel while dissecting a frog and stabs themself in the foot. Or worse, decides to stick it in somebody's neck.

Those are real possibilities. You don't tell the school they can't dissect frogs anymore." I can tell I'm getting away from myself here. But I can't stop. Steven would love this.

"I mean, some things are just going to happen whether we want them to or not. Nobody's to blame. We just got to do the best we can to get those situations under control and learn for the next time. Not look for somebody to hang out to dry."

"Whoa, wait a minute there," Mr. Dunn says. "That's not what we're doing here."

I try to get my thoughts back in line before I piss off Mr. Dunn for real and make this worse. "Sir, sorry. I just . . . I just wish you all could spend a week in Mr. Simmons' class. You wouldn't have any problem knowing what you should do. That's all."

The whole board stares at me. Some I think are happy about what I said, but a few with gray hair look like they want to put me in time-out. Or better yet, take me out to the woodshed. None of them say anything, so I sit back down.

"Damn Will," Samantha says, patting my leg when I sit down. "I didn't know you had it in you."

Neither Mrs. Teschner or Ms. Hartley get their wishes, which makes my stomach drop to my toes when they vote on Mr. Simmons.

Mr. Dunn says, "Those in favor of reinstating Mr. Jerry Simmons to the Coosa Creek High School faculty?"

Nobody is getting any favors tonight.

TWENTY-FIVE

Defeat makes an ugly picture. Mr. Simmons doesn't wait for the meeting to adjourn. He simply gets up and walks out like there isn't a living soul in the room, and that's about how much notice they give him. He ignores us all.

Just like my parents are doing to Steven. The house is absolutely silent when I get home.

"Kind of creepy, huh?" Steven is lying on his bed, reading a book for school, which is kind of funny since he won't be going tomorrow. But I wouldn't expect him to slack now.

"Yeah, still feels like a morgue in here," I agree.

"Neither one of them has said a word to me. I mean literally. Not a single syllable."

"Who picked you up from the school?"

"Mom made a rare appearance. I guess it was early enough, you know. And maybe she thought Dad would kill me right there in the office." He chuckles, the words falling out of his mouth like it would be hard for him to care any less. "Guess it's better than having a huge scene again."

"Is it?"

Steven shrugs one shoulder.

I know I'd rather have it out than be ignored. That just sucks you into a place where nothing you want to say or feel means a damn thing.

"Don't you care, even a little?"

"William, it's not a matter of whether I care. It's just the way things are. Wake up, man. This *is* the house we live in. Those people *are* our parents." He looks at me hard. I don't like the way he called them "those people."

He keeps on. "You act like this is all news or something. Accept it and get past it." He stops, his lips forming a slight smile. "It's a nice place to be."

Then he puts the book back in front of his face like that's the end of it. He can feel me still in the doorway, though. "William, go to bed. One of us has to get up for school."

I lay down, but sleep is only a distant idea that's being blocked by the barrage of other thoughts spinning around my head. I hear Daddy come in, and it's hard for me not to get up and go ask him why he won't talk to Steven.

I wallow in my own anger and desire until I have to throw off the covers and sit straight up in bed. So much doesn't make sense right now, which makes me ache to take comfort in the only thing that does.

━━━━

Destruction must come before resurrection. That much I know from sitting through hundreds of sermons. Is it something a nice guy would do? Probably not. Then again, Jesus wasn't *always* nice. But still, he was a hero, who was best at giving people second chances. Like me.

This time of night it doesn't take long to get to downtown, and it isn't hard not being seen. This place is quiet during the day, so in the middle of the night folks could run naked down the street and nobody would be the wiser.

I park my truck on the backside of the courthouse, the largest building in downtown Coosa Creek. With the full moon overhead, the four-story building casts a shadow that consumes everything within thirty yards. I walk along the sidewalk, hugging the concrete wall, stepping behind hedges that have gone too long without pruning. I stop at the corner of the building and stare across the street at the abandoned auto parts store.

It's a dead building with a dead man living inside. Nah, Leroy isn't actually dead, but to the folks here in Coosa Creek, he might as well be. They don't see him. And if they do, they pretend they don't. The way they see it is that it's Leroy's own fault. But tragedy changes that.

Most of my life I've heard folks around here complain on and on about people on welfare and how they can't believe their tax dollars are going to people who won't work. But that sure didn't keep the whole town from raising money for victims of the last hurricane to hit the Gulf Coast, and just about every church in Coosa Creek sent a group down there to help clean up and rebuild houses for the poor. No way they could let a disaster happen and not get involved. What they don't get is that we got plenty of disasters right here.

The thief comes only to steal and kill and destroy; I have come that they may have life, and have it to the fullest. — *John 10:10.*

I pull open the metal door and wait a couple minutes, listening for Leroy moving inside. When it's obvious the noise didn't wake him up, I click on my flashlight and step inside. I shine the light on the floor to keep from stepping on anything that might make enough noise to rouse old Leroy before I can get to him.

He's curled up in the same spot he was in earlier. His breathing is heavy and thick, the sound of being passed out that's as familiar as biscuits and jelly. I nudge him with my foot, but he doesn't even roll his head. I could probably do the Cotton-Eyed Joe on his head and he wouldn't know.

I lay my flashlight on the floor, take out some matches, and strike one. I light his oil lamp. It's bright in the pitch-black room. The change makes Leroy stir a little. I have to do this now.

I toss the lamp almost to the ceiling, toward the middle of the floor.

Glass shatters; oil splatters and ignites across the floor. Old auto parts boxes catch quick. Shreds of packing tape melt and crackle.

Leroy stirs more, his body trying to pull itself from the alcohol slumber his brain is floating in. I don't move an inch.

Smoke fills the room and crawls like morning fog over to me and Leroy. I drop to my knees to get some good air. The smoke makes Leroy cough a couple of times, and he finally opens his eyes.

He bolts upright, sees the flames, and scoots himself back against the wall. "Ahh, Lord have mercy." He sees me. "What's going on in here?"

"Leroy, remember me?"

He just stares back at me, half-dazed, half-terrified.

"I saw the smoke. I'm going to get you out of here."

I grab his arm and pull, but he doesn't budge. "Come on, this place is going up fast."

I pull again. He fights against me like a stubborn mule. I lean hard backwards to get him away from the wall. He only slides an inch on the dusty concrete floor.

The flames and heat spread.

"Leroy, this isn't a game, man. Do you want to die?" And then it occurs to me that maybe he does. But I'm not going to let him.

I release his arm and grab his coat collar with both hands. I jerk him off the floor. He's much lighter than I expected. He fights me, hitting and pushing at my shoulders and chest.

"Just leave me be. Just leave me be."

He drops his legs out from under himself like a two-year-old throwing a tantrum in the grocery store.

I hold tight and try to pick him back up, but it's pretty clear he's not going to let that happen. So I do the only thing I can. I let go of his collar, lean over, and plant my right shoulder into his gut. I wrap my arms around his back and heave him up over my shoulder like a sack of corn.

Leroy pounds my back with his fists, but he can beat my kidneys into oblivion for all I care. I'm not putting him down.

I turn toward the space of concrete that has turned into a field of flames and smoke. I pick a route where the flames are lowest.

I am not afraid.

"Baptized with fire," I say out loud, and take off.

Leroy bounces and screams as I run through flames kissing my legs and my bare hands latched onto Leroy's legs. Through the smoke I can see light shining out the back door. I high-step the last fifteen feet and fall through the door, both of us skidding across the gravel.

I jump up and check Leroy. He rolls on the ground, his hair and old coat smoking but no flames. He tucks both of his hands to his chest. I look down at my jeans. The bottoms are singed black, and I can smell the burned soles of my boots. Scorched rubber and hair would make a woodchuck chuck, but right now it's as good as a kitchen on Thanksgiving morning.

Behind me, the fire almost reaches a roar. Blue lights flash around the corner of the building. Leroy coughs on the ground.

"Here, let me get you up." I help him sit up so he can breathe better.

He coughs a few more times, then looks me dead in the eye. "Why didn't you just leave me be?"

"I'm just not that kind of guy."

I pat his shoulder and help him to his feet. We walk around the corner of the building to where a police car is parked in the middle of Main Street. Sirens sound in the distance.

The cop runs toward us. "Jesus H. Christ, were the two of you in there? Come on now, get back." He pushes both of us across the street to the sidewalk by the court-house. "Sit down."

We both sit on the curb.

"What were you doing in there?" he asks me.

"I saw the smoke. Knew Leroy stayed in there." I cough a couple times.

The cop looks at Leroy. "Crazy old coot. Could have got this boy killed." He shakes his head. Leroy nearly about coughs his lungs out. The cop grabs his radio and calls for an ambulance. When he clips his radio back on his belt, the tanker and brush-fire truck pull up to the front of the store.

There's no hope for the building, which is just what I wanted. Only a concrete slab.

Marcus Wombley and Seth Parker get a line hooked

up to the hydrant on the corner. Billy pulls the hose off the brush-fire truck and starts spraying the roof where flames sprout into the sky.

Chief Griffin sees Leroy and me sitting on the sidewalk. He shakes his head but ignores us otherwise. I'm sure not for long, though. So it occurs to me I might want to have an explanation.

The Chief grabs a fire ax and busts out the front windows so Marcus can have a clear shot inside. Nobody moves too fast. No point really. The important part has already been done.

An ambulance pulls up within a few minutes. The EMTs come over with their bags. It's the same two guys who showed up at the car fire. This town is as short on medics as we are on firemen.

One of them looks at me. He recognizes my face. "Good Lord, boy, are you psychic, or do you just carry disaster wherever you go?"

"I don't know," is all I can say.

"Maybe he's a guardian angel," Chief Griffin says, behind them.

The EMT turns his head for a second and then looks back at me. "You okay?"

"I'm fine," I say, even though I can feel my ankles burning and the backs of my hands pulsing where I know blisters will be tomorrow. "But here, check Leroy out."

Leroy has both hands tucked into his armpits. He still

coughs from the smoke, or maybe it's the whiskey and wine. Either way, he needs them more than I do.

They lift him off the curb and walk him toward the ambulance. Chief Griffin steps over and sits down.

"Heck of a fire."

"Yeah."

Chief Griffin rubs his hands together. "So, William, how did you get here before we did?"

"Couldn't sleep, you know. Just got a lot going on. Driving helps me sort things out. You know how some people have their best ideas in the shower? Well, mine are behind the wheel." I'm talking too fast, so I take a breath. "So anyway. Saw the smoke. I knew Leroy stayed in there. Everybody knows."

"Hhmm." Chief Griffin stops rubbing his hands together and strokes his beard. "Where's your truck?"

"I parked over there," I point around the side of the building. "Far away from the fire."

"I see." Chief is quiet for a few seconds. "Just driving around, huh?"

"Yeah, I like coming through here sometimes. You know, just often enough that I don't forget what it looks like. Guess I picked a good night."

"Well, it's going to look a little different now." Chief Griffin looks across the street at the fire that's under control but will still finish the job. "So, why didn't you put your gear on?"

"Chief, I know that was stupid. I wasn't thinking." It's the truth. I should have thought about that.

"Well, could you tell how it started?"

"No telling. So much booze in the air in there a cigarette would set it off. Not the safest place."

Chief Griffin waves his hand over toward the back of the ambulance where Leroy's getting his hands wrapped in gauze. "He's been in this building for years. Heck, he's almost been here longer than the stop sign. Wonder what he's going to do now?" His voice is actually concerned.

"Aw, I'm sure some folks will help him out. This wasn't his fault."

"How you know?"

"Just a gut feeling, I guess."

"Well, I have a feeling your gut is right."

I don't look at the Chief. I keep my eyes on Leroy. The EMTs help him all the way into the back of the ambulance and lay him on the stretcher. At least for tonight, he'll sleep on a mattress. Nurses will feed him, check on him, and treat him like any other patient.

"It usually is."

TWENTY-SIX

Protests seem more like Samantha's thing than mine, but I have to do something. I can't just walk into fifth period physics like everything is fine and dandy. So I do the only thing I can. When the bell rings to change classes, I walk right out of the school, get in my truck, and drive off.

In Coosa Creek, there aren't many places to hide. I only know of one place that's almost guaranteed to be deserted.

The firehouse isn't empty like I hoped. Chief Griffin's truck sets out front. He might say something about me not being in school, so I should probably turn around and find somewhere else. But when you get down to it, I got nowhere to go right now and gas isn't cheap. I'll take my chances.

The door doesn't make a sound when I open it and step into the firehouse, which is really just a metal building with two bay doors, a regular door, and two windows you could barely squeeze a poodle through. The Chief's not sitting at his desk, so I walk around the front of the tanker. I can hear him but I can't see him. I call, "Chief?"

Something metal bangs on the concrete floor, and Chief Griffin peeks his head around the back of the brush-fire truck. "Good Lord, William, you nearly made me have to go clean out my drawers." He rubs his hand over his face. "That's what I get for putting all that WD-40 on them hinges. I can't hear nobody coming."

"Sorry, Chief."

He disappears behind the back of the truck and picks up the wrench he dropped. "What you doing here? Ain't you supposed to be in school still?"

"Well, sir, I kind of had to leave early today."

He walks up to the side of the truck and stares me down. "Had to or wanted to?" He raises an eyebrow at me. "You wouldn't be playing hooky, would you?" He's not pissed, so I don't have any reason to lie to him.

"I guess that's one way of putting it."

"Now, I can't have my men getting into trouble. When Seth Parker started with us, I had to make him swear off going down to the Broke Spoke. That boy just couldn't keep his mouth shut and his hands to himself."

"Oh, you don't have to worry about me, Chief. I don't drink or nothing."

"William, don't get smart. You know what I mean."

"Yes, sir. I just needed a little time is all."

"Uh-hmm." Chief Griffin sets the wrench on the truck and shoves his hands in his pockets. "Come on over and take a load off."

I follow him over to his desk. He plops down in his squeaky chair and I sit on the old sofa. It's covered with cigarette burns and stains that I don't even want to guess where they came from.

"So what's eating at you?"

"Me, sir? I'm fine."

"Well, you said you left school 'cause you need some time. Something got to be eating you."

I know Chief Griffin will understand. "Just the thing with Mr. Simmons."

"Oh, I hear you. All that's just a damn shame. In fact, he's why I'm here. Called me to meet him so he could drop off his gear." Chief Griffin points over to a pile on the floor. "So I just decided to stick around and do some tinkering."

"You made him quit?"

"Nope. All on his own."

"But... did he say why?"

"Didn't ask. But I'm sure it's got something to do with that Trahan boy and then them folks taking his job." Chief starts rocking in his chair. "I tried to talk him out of it. Told him he needed to do *something* until he could get another position somewhere. Get him out of the house at least before he drove poor Janet crazy. It can get pretty scary if a man don't feel like he's of some use."

"Yeah."

"Heck, why you think my old bones is still messing with all this? If I don't feel like I'm doing something useful, I just wither up and die. Or the missus might end up killing me with a shovel. I know Jerry's like that. That's why it worries me, him just coming in here and quitting like he done. It seemed way too easy."

I look at the floor and shake my head. "It was just an accident. Wrong place, wrong time."

"Yep, some things we just don't have a say in. Speaking of, you seem to have the opposite affliction."

"Sir?"

"You've seen quite a lot of action here recently, haven't you?"

"I don't know. Not sure what a lot is, really."

"Oh, seems like you have a gift for being in the right place at the right time."

"That's not a bad thing."

"No, not at all. But be careful. Doing this can get way under your skin, like I've told you. Make you forget stuff, important stuff you ain't supposed to ever forget. We all have to deal with it. Those of us who've been doing this for a while, whether we want to get down and admit it, love it 'cause it gives us a feeling that can't be matched, not even by sex." He looks all serious at me. "You know what I'm talking about?"

"I'll just have to take your word for it, Chief."

He leans forward and shuffles through some papers on his desk. "I need you to take a look at something." He picks up a sheet and hands it across his desk. "Here you go."

I take the sheet and read the top. "Incident report."

"I've been meaning to show that to you."

I keep reading the words, written in Chief Griffin's almost pretty handwriting. Even though he's claimed time and time again it's his wife's handwriting, all of us on the team know better.

The report is about the fire behind the D&G.

While I read, Chief Griffin says, "Whenever there's a fire that was set instead of being an accident, I got to fill one of those out, do an investigation. Just like I'm doing with the church fire."

"Right." I finish reading and set the paper down. "You got any leads?"

"That's where you come in."

"Me?" My throat nearly closes shut.

"I'm pretty sure it was a kid, probably somebody at the school."

"How you figure?" I get the words out without sounding like I'm out of breath.

"Just call it old fireman's instincts. I mean, a real fire-setter would have set fire to the building. That fire was more like a prank. But one we can't have happen again. From what I've read, setting fires is about as addictive as putting them out. Folks will eventually get hurt. So you just keep your ears open. One thing about kids is, they can't keep their damn mouths shut for nothing." He holds his hands out. "No offense."

I shake my head. "None taken, Chief."

"There will be talk. So you just listen up."

"Yes, sir." I look down at my watch. "Well, Chief, I got to be getting to work."

"That's right, you do work down there at the D&G, don't you?"

"Almost every day."

"You ain't got nothing you want to tell me about, do you?" He pauses and stares. "I mean, you didn't see nobody messing around the back of the store?"

"Not that I recall, but I'll let you know if I remember something."

"You do that." Chief Griffin gets up out of his chair. "Well, I got to get over to Mr. Thornton's with the brush-fire truck. The two of us are going to do a controlled burn over in some of his pines." He kind of laughs but it's not really a laugh. "That's funny, controlled burn. There's two words that don't go together."

TWENTY-SEVEN

"You're officially trying to get thrown out of school for good, aren't you?" I say.

Samantha is back at her post on the sidewalk in front of the school with another cardboard box. No condoms, just pamphlets on the correct use of condoms.

"Will, I'm not going to be censored."

"You'll get five-day suspension instead of two this time, I'm telling you."

"If that's what it takes."

I look at Steven, appealing for some assistance. "Hey, man, the girl gets an idea in her head," he says.

"Don't I know it."

I snatch up the box. "Well, I'm not going to let you do this."

Samantha drops the pamphlets in her hand and latches onto the box. "Will, don't play with me."

What I'd like to tell her is that I'm a little overwhelmed with all the shit both her and Steven are heaping on me right now. But I figure that won't get me too far.

"Look, I have a better idea, if you'll just let go."

She's suspicious, but lets go anyway.

"All right. What?"

I hand her half of the brochures.

"The rest, please?"

"Nope. You put those in the girls' bathroom and I'll put these in the boys'. That way, you get them out and also keep from getting suspended again."

"That's kind of the wimp's way out, don't you think?"

"Yeah, but it sucks here without you."

She smiles big at me. "Thanks."

Thank God that's what she needed to hear, because we could have argued all morning.

I watch her go toward the front entrance with that long, confident walk that says, "Follow or get out of the way."

"Steven, between the two of you, I'm going to be stark-raving nuts in no time."

———

The condom caper continued without incident. Samantha made it through the day without getting called into the office, although I could tell at lunch she wasn't too happy about not hand-delivering each and every pamphlet. I don't care if she's a bit upset with me, because sometimes people have to be saved from themselves. That's a reality I've come to accept with her. And it's even more clear when I meet up with Steven after school.

He stands out next to the bus lane waving his homecoming pictures in the air like he's trying to signal a rescue plane. The pictures were handed out in sixth period, but since Samantha paid for ours, she got them instead of me. I'm sure I won't be duplicating Steven's excitement when I see mine.

"Well, from the looks of your reaction, I guess you like the way they turned out," I say.

"Here, look."

Steven hands me the envelope. I have to break the seal, so I know I'm the first to see them. I slide out the five-by-seven. It would be a lie to say the picture doesn't make me a little uncomfortable, but I love my brother. I don't let him see it.

"So, what do you think?"

"They turned out really well. You make a good match."

Steven takes the picture and envelope from me. "Well, not as good a match as I thought."

"Huh?"

"Yep, Buck dropped me like a used condom."

"Steven, give me a break."

"Sorry, after seeing those brochures, I've been waiting all day to use that."

"What happened?" The only reason I ask is because I know Steven wants to say it out loud.

"He just couldn't handle it. At least, not right now. Not here, this school, this town." Steven puts the picture back in the envelope. "He said I scare him."

"Steven, I hate to say it, but I kind of agree with him on that."

"Yeah, I know." He doesn't try to make me feel better, doesn't tell me not to worry because he knows that around here, there's plenty to worry about. "But at least I made it through the week without getting my face smashed in again." He smiles like this is a victory of some kind.

"Yeah, well..." I stop there because this wasn't a normal week—the condom parade, Steven being gone for a couple days.

"So..." Steven brightens up. "How do you think the picture will look on the mantle, or maybe the refrigerator?"

"You're kidding, right?"

"I'm afraid not, little brother."

"I think it might be one picture too many. You know, things are kind of crowded like they are."

"Yeah, but they won't be able to ignore this."

Steven's comment makes me think of what Samantha said—if people don't talk about it then they can act like it doesn't exist. "Well, if you're ready for the madness, then I guess I am too."

The chaos, however, beats me home. While I drifted in the fluorescent cloud and quiet of Friday night at the D&G, Steven and Mom were both finally acknowledged—loud, clear, and hard.

Every picture on the refrigerator is torn to pieces and lying on the kitchen floor, a chair is broken, and shattered glass covers the counter.

"Hey," I call into the house, still gazing at the mess. "Everybody okay?"

"In here, William," Steven's calm voice comes from the living room. I tiptoe around to see over to the couch. Steven and Mom sit together, not touching but at least close. No glass sits in front of her or fills her hand. Tears glisten on her cheeks.

"What happened?"

"Dad didn't like my homecoming picture."

"Yeah, I kind of figured. But the chair, the glass?"

"It was the chair's fault. It got in my way when Dad pretty much threw me across the room."

"You all right?"

"I just wanted him to stop ripping up pictures."

Mom lets out a whimper. "Ones when he was little. He just tore them up." She cries a little harder.

I wait for Steven to answer my question. But he doesn't.

"The glass, well..." His head motions toward Mom,

and I realize she's probably crying just as much about the loss of her beverage as the pictures.

"Did he hit you?" I ask Mom.

She shakes her head.

"You?"

"The chair did it for him," Steven says. "But he finally said something again."

"And what was that?"

"That I have to leave."

Mom casts her eyes down to the floor. Shame is an awful thing to look at. I figure maybe she tried to defend Steven. That's how come Daddy broke her glass. But her fighting him was about as successful as her fighting against the bottle.

"Where is he?"

"Guess."

TWENTY-EIGHT

From the door I can hear Daddy preaching with passion and heat to the empty pews. His voice echoes with such conviction it makes me nervous. I've no idea what I'm going to say, but something has got to be said, got to be done.

Daddy doesn't see or hear me come in by the organ at the front of the church. He stops to take a couple of breaths, flips a page of his notes for Sunday, and turns a page in the giant Bible on top of the pulpit. That Bible used to scare me when I was really little. It looked like a huge book of magical spells. Daddy would read the words. Some people would cry, some would raise their hands in praise. I didn't understand all the words, still don't, but I knew they were powerful. And my whole life he used them like a weapon—to make Steven and me do right, to try to explain the unexplainable, to defend the faith that's guided his life.

"I hope Sunday's sermon is about forgiveness," I say pretty loud.

Daddy jerks his head up and finds me standing off to the side of the stage. "This is a surprise. Aren't you supposed to be at work still?" He looks down at his watch to see that it's much later than he thought. "What you doing up here, son?"

"Being my brother's keeper." I figure it's the right thing to say for the location, the situation.

Daddy drops his head and stares at the pages of the Bible. "Well, you're going to have to be, because we can't keep him anymore." He looks over at the organ, and I know he's thinking Steven won't be playing this Sunday.

"'Let he who is without sin cast the first stone.'" There is only way to argue with my daddy, even if I feel like I'm using a slingshot against a bazooka.

Daddy looks hard at me. "'If a man also lie with mankind, as he lies with woman, both of them have committed an abomination.'"

"'This is my commandment, that you love one another as I have loved you.'"

Daddy shakes his head. "Do you think I don't love your brother? I love him enough to show him the errors of his ways."

I've often thought about Daddy's contradictions but

never made mention of them. Guess this is as good a time as any.

"And what about drunkenness?" I look right at him. "Who is worse, do you think? The drunk? Or the one who can help the drunk but doesn't? Which one is more of an abomination?"

Daddy slams the Bible shut. "This is not about … "

"Do you know what abomination means? It isn't sin, you know."

He steps down off the stage and walks toward me. "Don't tell me … "

"It means dislike."

He grabs a handful of my shirt. But I'm not going to stop. Daddy has never listened—to me, Mom, or Steven.

"What have *you* done that God dislikes?"

"Shut up." Daddy grips my shirt harder and shakes me.

"But he still lets you in his house."

Daddy shoves me back. I catch myself against the first pew.

"You're too young to understand," he says.

"Maybe so, but it could be just the opposite, Daddy. Maybe I'm young enough to understand. Could be that I see all this like it is. And you have to sift it through too much life and too much worry about what people will think."

He looks at me with nothing to say.

"Daddy, you can't just put him out."

He doesn't reply, but I keep looking at him waiting for him to say what I want to hear. But I know that only happens when he stands behind that pulpit. Something about him coming down those steps transforms him, just as much as the whiskey and gin transforms my mother.

It doesn't take long to realize he's not going to budge. Just too far of a leap for him to make.

I look behind him at the baptismal font and remember when I stood there when I was twelve with Daddy's hand on my shoulder. For the whole week leading up to that day, I must have heard the words "forgiveness," "renewal," and "rebirth" a hundred times. When he pulled me up out of the water, it was the one time I knew he was really proud of me. And I wish like everything I could be proud of him. Just maybe...

The end of a matter is better than its beginning, and patience is better than pride. —Ecclesiastes 7:8.

TWENTY-NINE

I know I shouldn't be surprised that Samantha's parents said it was okay for Steven to stay there until we got things sorted out. I mean, she's their offspring. But I was baffled at them acting like it wasn't even something to consider for more than two seconds. They were all too happy, which is much more than I can say for Samantha when I wake her up at seven a.m.

"You better have a really good reason to call me this early. Like the solution to world peace or something."

"I won't go that far," I say, "but it's pretty good."

"I'm hanging up now," she muffles into the phone.

"It has something to do with Leroy."

That gets her attention. Then I explain, sort of, what happened at the auto parts store and tell her if she wants to do something, the two of them have to meet me at the Waffle Hut before I go into work.

━━━━━

"You know I blame you for this, right?" I say.

"Me? I didn't burn the building down," Samantha retorts.

The three of us sit at a table at the Waffle Hut. The place is packed because it's Saturday morning and grease is a favorite fuel for the weekend around here.

"Not for the situation, Mother Teresa. This idea I have—it's sort of an extension of your project."

"And why exactly did I have to get up for this?" Steven says.

"Well, my fine brother, you've got the most important part."

"All right, let's hear it."

"Here's the way I see it. When the Ehlers' house mostly burned down, folks at church emptied their pockets the next Sunday morning like the money was burning a hole in them. And the Ehlers still had insurance and a relative to stay with and all. Leroy's got nothing. People have been ignoring him forever, but now the two of you are going to make sure they see him—up close and in color."

Samantha's face perks up.

"Your phone shoots video, right?"

"Yeah. Well, it's not good video, but it works."

"It doesn't have to be good, don't worry."

"So what am I recording?"

"I want ya'll to go over to the hospital. Samantha, you talk to Leroy about where he's from, how he got to be homeless, what it's been like for him. Real sob stuff. Steven, you'll video."

Samantha jumps in. "What if he won't talk to me? He was, you know, a little rough around the edges last time."

"He was plowed, Samantha. Kind of makes a difference. Now he's not."

"I guess."

"Look, I already called and made sure he's there. He's in room 1237. See, done some of the work for you."

"So, okay. We go talk to him and video what he says. That's it?"

"Not quite."

"Well, then tell me quite."

I turn to Steven. "You're going to show it during tomorrow's eleven o'clock service."

"I'm going to do WHAT?" Steven's voice makes everybody turn and look. He lowers his voice. "William, whatever fumes you inhaled in the last fire cooked your synapses or something."

"You're not going to be playing the organ, so you can just go in the back, load the video, turn on the projector, and hit the button for the screen to come down. Simple."

"He's going to have a complete fit. You know that."

"He could, but it won't be until after church, and you get to leave. I'll have to deal with it. That's why I'm not doing it myself. One of us has to pull this family back together. But this isn't about Daddy. It's about Leroy and seeing if those people will put their money where their mouths are."

"Well," Samantha says, "I'm game."

"Hang on, there's one more thing. Samantha, I need you to go to the church with Steven."

"Are you serious? I might kind of stick out a little, don't you think?" She points to her brown skin. "I'm sure I wouldn't be too far off to assume you don't have many of us at your church."

"Eh, don't worry about that. Nobody will say anything even if they're thinking it."

"What do you want me to do?"

"When the video is over, just walk up to the front and read this." I pull a sheet of paper out of my pocket and hand it to her.

She unfolds and reads: "'For I was hungry, and you gave me meat; I was thirsty, and you gave me drink; I was a stranger, and you took me in; naked, and you clothed me.'"

"They won't be able to stand it, something like that getting put right in their faces. Some of them folks will feel like if they don't do something they'll never be able to darken the doorstep of the church again."

"Why are you doing this?"

"Some people just deserve better. A chance, at least."

THIRTY

You who are young, be happy while you are young, and let your heart give you joy in the days of your youth. —Ecclesiastes 11:9.

This just verifies how some things are worth it. Our little stunt worked better than I could have hoped—a lot of pockets got lighter, and Daddy didn't even try to kill Samantha when she read her piece. He played it off like he'd planned it all himself. And that made people talk about other things they could do for Leroy. I guess they see winning points with Pastor Tucker as like winning favor with God himself.

And I swear DJ would say his pain was worth it, that it

wasn't too bad a price for what he gets to experience now. The whole student body is packed in the gym—many wearing their orange bracelets proudly—for the special assembly Mr. Edwards called to welcome DJ back.

Our principal stands at a podium in the middle of the basketball court. He gives a hand signal over to the door of the gym and in comes Mandy, pushing DJ in a wheelchair. The huge room erupts into applause like their favorite band just took the stage. Mandy and DJ both smile like this is the finest moment of their lives. Mandy, with her makeup-less face and plain clothes, positions the chair next to the podium.

"Today, students, we are here to celebrate." Everybody starts clapping again and Mr. Edwards waits for the applause to stop before he goes on. "We're not just celebrating the return of a student, but also the kindness and support he received from all of you. Today I am proud to be your principal. And all of you need to be proud of yourselves." He stops and unfolds a piece of paper. "As of last Friday, because of the efforts of Indians in Action and the generosity of this student body and the Coosa Creek community, we have raised nearly $10,000 for Paul."

The crowd goes crazy, like this is a pep rally. Mr. Edwards is really having a good time with this. He beams. Once the noise drops below ear-splitting, he looks over at DJ. "Would you like to say a few words?"

DJ shakes his head. I guess he doesn't know what he could say to all this, except "Thank you."

Mr. Edward nods and turns back to the mike. "Before we wrap this up and get back to class, I have one more person I'd like to recognize. And I guess I should have already done this, but better late than never." He scans the crowd for a few seconds. "I'd like William Tucker to stand up, please."

People around me pat my back, prodding me. Samantha elbows me. "Go ahead, hero." When I stand up, I get the same reaction DJ got when he entered the gym. And I have to admit, I feel like a hero. It's a perfect moment.

I sit quickly, and more hands pat and nudge me like I'm their best friend. It is crazy to think all of this came from a single spark.

Mr. Edwards says a few more words I don't pay attention to and then dismisses us. People move about as slow as grass growing, prolonging this and shortening their time in class as much as possible. We get jostled around in the crowd as we leave.

Samantha manages to turn around. "Hey, you going with Steven and me this afternoon?"

"Wish I could." She's going to see Leroy in the hospital again. He didn't suffer any real injuries from the fire, but they found a heap of other problems when they got him in there.

"Oh, come on, don't you want to see his face when we tell him about the church?" she asks.

"I got to work and do some stuff."

"All right, have it your way," Samantha says before the crowd pushes her away and out the door.

If positive energy was a physical thing, I'd have to wade to class like I was pushing through knee-deep Alabama mud. But in the midst of it all, I have to drop my head and mourn the absence of Mr. Simmons. Some people do deserve better.

THIRTY-ONE

I figure the best thing in the world to do for someone who thinks he's lost his whole life is to make him feel like it's been given back to him. That's why I can do this.

Fire can fix it.

I know that Mr. Simmons' driveway is long, winding through pecan trees that nearly hide the house from the road. Like most folks that live out this way, he's planted reflectors at the end of the driveway so people trying to get to his house don't blow right by.

I park my truck about thirty yards short of those reflectors. I get out on the edge of the dark, deserted road a little after midnight. I put my gear on except for my helmet and fire boots. They'll just slow me down.

The walk up the driveway is a bit creepy with the shadows of the trees looking like skeleton arms reaching down to grab me. I walk fast, in the grass so my feet don't make noise on the gravel. It's quiet and peaceful out here. Almost makes me sorry to have to ruin it.

The driveway comes up over a mound right in front of the house. The place is an old-style ranch home with a raised wooden porch, concrete steps, swing, and two rocking chairs. It's the kind of place people up North see in magazines and think that every house in the South looks just like it. Not fancy, just simple and lived-in.

I ease up to the porch and get on my knees. I reach into the pockets of my fire jacket and unload the pine straw crammed in there. Dry pine straw is almost as good as gasoline.

When I get the straw arranged in a nice pile underneath the porch, I dig in my pocket for the camp flint and steel. I figure the very tool that started this thing for Mr. Simmons should also give him another chance.

Without even hesitating, I strike the flint across the steel with a hard blow. Sparks fly into the pile of straw. Slight traces of smoke drift up. I strike again, and again, and again, three quick times. The straw is so dry it doesn't smoke much, just a few whiffs and the pile transforms into the sun.

I wait a second to make sure all of it is going to catch, and then turn and haul butt back to my truck.

When I climb in behind the steering wheel, I can see flickers through the trees. As the fire grows, so do the shadows of the trees across the ground. I stare at my pager sitting on the seat next to me. It's going to go off soon.

Two minutes, nothing.

Three. Still nothing.

Four.

I look up at the house, and the fire has migrated across the whole porch. The trees are not shadows anymore. The light is bright enough to see the bark.

I pick up my pager and shake it. "Come on." I can't do anything until I hear sirens in the distance.

And then the beeps blare inside the truck. "Finally!"

I roll down my window so I can hear the sirens coming. I can't be too early on this one.

The crackle of the fire in the distance covers up the night sounds. But I listen hard, waiting, the agony of my impatience growing every second. My left leg starts bouncing up and down like that's going to make the trucks get here faster.

The clock on the radio shows I've been waiting six minutes. It doesn't sound like long, but fires can eat like alligators.

My hand is slippery on the key. I wipe it on the seat. I stick my head out the window, still trying to catch the sirens coming this way.

Then, through the darkness, I hear that faint song of the siren giving me the go-ahead. I sling dirt and rocks and squeal tires down the road to get into Mr. Simmons' driveway. Going toward the house, cutting around the curves, the back of my truck fishtails, nearly clipping the pecan trees that crowd the way.

When I slam on the brakes in front of the house, Mrs. Simmons stands outside one of the windows. Smoke alarms blare inside. Over the noise, I hear Mr. Simmons yell at her from inside, "Get back, get back."

A chair comes flying through the glass. Clothes come soon after. Then picture frames. Mr. Simmons should know better, but I knew he would do this. Folks just can't help it. They have to cling on to any shred of their old life they can get their hands on.

I grab my boots out of the back, pull them on, and throw on my helmet. The fire has completely engulfed the porch and most of the front of the house. I run up to Mrs. Simmons, who's standing way too close to the house, and wrap my arms around her.

"You got to get back to a safe distance, ma'am."

She doesn't even acknowledge I'm here.

I don't tell her again. I just pick her up and run back toward my truck.

"Let me go, let me go," she screams, whacking me much the same way Leroy did. Some folks just don't know what's good for them.

I drop her on the grass, but she pops right back up like I

put her down on a trampoline. She tries to run back toward the window that's now pouring out smoke like an old freight train. I get my hands around her enough to hold her back.

"Ma'am, you got to stay back."

Her arms and legs windmill a few more times before she gives up.

"Just sit down."

She starts to sob.

Red and white lights flash through the trees as the trucks turn into the driveway. I have to move fast. I don't want anybody taking this from me.

"I'll get him, ma'am. I'll be right back."

I charge at the window that Mr. Simmons busted out, call his name a couple of times. But he doesn't reply. I grab the windowsill with both hands, squat and hurl myself halfway through the window on top of the broken pane. Thank God my jacket is just about tough enough to take a gunshot.

I squirm through the window, staying glued to the floor. The fire has made it into the hallway. I crawl on my stomach, smoke floating just above my back.

"Mr. Simmons," I call. "Mr. Simmons."

I use my forearms to work my way around the foot of the bed and find Mr. Simmons on the floor in front of the closet in his boxers and a white T-shirt, unconscious. I take his arm and shake it, but he doesn't move. I pull myself closer to him and shake both this shoulders. Nothing.

The heat from the hallway bears down on my back. I

look over my shoulder to see the flames pulling themselves through the doorway. I have to wake Mr. Simmons up. He needs to see this, how close the flames are. I need him to feel how close all of this is. He's got to know what he's escaping.

I roll Mr. Simmons over on his side and shake him again. "Wake up now, Mr. Simmons. Wake up."

The house creaks and moans like a monster as the fire makes it into the bedroom. I can hear water already hitting the front of the house.

I roll Mr. Simmons back toward me and tuck my hands under his armpits to lift him. I get his body in a seated position, but his head just falls forward. He isn't going to see this part. That's really too bad. I just hope it doesn't make a difference.

I move around behind him and lift him off the floor. He's way heavier than old Leroy. Two steps back I set him on the edge of the bed so I can get him up on my shoulder. It takes everything I got. I don't know how much he weighs, but I can't imagine a refrigerator weighs much more.

I stumble around the end of the bed and fix my eyes on the window. I can see water reflecting the lights against the black night. I take a deep breath and shoot forward as fast as I can and jump out the window.

In midair I have the same feeling I had that time I jumped off the roof of the house—pure exhilaration. Water splashing off the house sprays my burning face, and it's as good as anything I've ever felt.

When my feet hit the ground, I let Mr. Simmons'

weight topple me over and both of us skid across the now-wet grass. I pull my arms out from under his body and yell, "Oxygen. Need some oxygen over here."

Billy Parker comes running with the green tank. He kneels down next to Mr. Simmons and presses the clear plastic mask over his mouth. With about ten seconds of the pure oxygen, Mr. Simmons opens his eyes. And I'm right here to greet him.

"You're all right. No dying tonight."

His eyes dart around, lost, until his wife falls on the ground next to him. She doesn't say anything. She just leans over and starts kissing his cheek over and over like he's been gone for years. Mr. Simmons closes his eyes, nods, and reaches over to pat the back of his wife's head. He's not sad. He's grateful. They both are.

THIRTY-TWO

I would say the sun coming through the window wakes me, if I was actually asleep. But I didn't sleep a wink all night. I just lay there staring at the inside of my eyelids, enjoying the anticipation of things to come and soaking up the satisfaction of what's been done.

It was hard seeing Mr. Simmons watch his house go down like that, the helplessness written across his forehead like a scripture I was forced to read so I could understand the pain he'll have to endure.

Before I left, he put both arms around me and said, "God bless you, William."

"No sir, he's blessed you."

He nodded at me. "Kind of hard to feel that way right now, though."

"Yeah. Things can't be undone, but they sure can be redone."

He actually smirked a little. "Just makes me tired thinking about it."

"Tired's better than dead."

He nodded again and looked over at his wife, who was getting in their neighbor's truck. "I'll have to remember that."

"Guess ya'll are taken care of for tonight."

"Yeah, but tomorrow I don't know." Mr. Simmons turned and walked toward the truck where Mrs. Simmons was waiting.

"Well, word will get around. And don't underestimate the power of sympathy with folks around here. Surprises me all the time."

He just held his hand up and waved without turning around.

I'm watching that wave in my head when the gravel crunches under tires outside. I peek out the window to see Chief Griffin's truck. I don't know why he's here this time of day, but I get up and pull on jeans and a sweatshirt.

When I walk into the hallway, Daddy has already let Chief Griffin in. But Daddy doesn't say anything to me. He just looks my way and says, "There he is."

I'd like to yell back at him, "Yeah, here I am!" because he's taken up ignoring me more than he ever has. Since

Sunday, he's treated me like an apparition, a cloudy indication that maybe he isn't the father he thought he was. At least that's the way he looks at me.

"Good morning, William," Chief Griffin says. "I hate stirring up folks at the crack, but I figured you'd be getting up for school anyway." He looks down at my feet. "Throw on some shoes and a jacket and come take a ride with me."

"Sir?"

"Come on, need you to help me with something."

Chief knows I don't ever turn anybody down when they ask for help. When I first asked him about joining the volunteer fire department, he said it was the one thing that let him know I'd be a good one to have on board.

"Give me just a second," I say.

━━━━━

The ride the Chief takes me on goes right to the end of Mr. Simmons' driveway. He doesn't even pull over to the side of the road. He just stops, turns on his hazards and wig-wags and says, "Get out and let me show you something."

We both get out, and I follow the Chief to the back of his truck. He points to the asphalt where there's a long black streak extending from where my truck was parked last night.

"I didn't notice it last night, but when I came over here this morning to take a fresh look in the light of day, it jumped right out at me."

"Okay," I say, like I don't understand why this is such a big deal.

"Now William, I know boys are burning tires all over these roads, but this one here is special."

"How's that, sir?"

"Get back in the truck. This is just the start of today's lesson."

Chief Griffin goes up the driveway and parks in front of what is left of the Simmons' house. About the only discernible feature is the concrete steps that look almost like a tombstone without the house around them.

"Things sure look different in the daylight, don't they?"

"Yes, sir, they do."

"I guess it's good most of our calls are at night. Makes it easier when you ain't got to see this stuff up close. But not today. Come on."

Chief gets out of the truck and I follow. "Now, that tire mark in the middle of the road don't mean much by itself," he says as he walks to where the porch used to be. "But when you add this on top of it, well, then we got something interesting."

He stops and looks down at his feet. "Take a look at this."

I step over next to him. At his feet is a black circle that's just a shade or two darker than the ground around it.

"Here's where it started." He squats down and runs his fingers across the dirt. His fingers pinch the ground. He blows on his finger to remove some dirt. "See, this here is a piece of pine straw." He looks at it real close. "You can just barely tell it, but that's what it is, for sure." He looks across the charred remains. "Amazing. Fire like that and this stuff don't completely disappear."

Chief Griffin drops the burnt pieces and rubs his hands together. Without standing back up, he says, "Now, the funny thing is, Jerry ain't got a pine tree within a hundred yards of this place. Nothing but all them pecans." He puts his hands on his knees and pushes himself back to standing.

"So what's this got to do with the tire mark?" Playing dumb is all I can do.

"Glad you asked. Like to see you staying on top of things, William." He faces the road like he's deliberately avoiding eye contact with me. "Now, I'd bet a free dinner down at Aunt Jenny's Catfish House that the tire mark down on the road there was left by the person who set this fire."

"Set?"

"Oh, yes sir. No doubt about it."

"Nobody around here would do that."

"Would, and did, just like the fire behind the D&G, at your daddy's church, the one at the old auto parts store, and now this." Chief doesn't even stop for me to reply. "See, at first I thought that fire behind the grocery store was a prank. But now I think it was practice."

"Chief, I'm not saying you're wrong, but you're making a few mighty big leaps."

"Yeah, William, you might be right. Hell, I hope you are. But I been putting out fires in Coosa Creek for forty years. And I ain't ever had this many fires this close together. The town just ain't that exciting."

"Times could be changing."

"Oh, for some, they sure will be."

Chief Griffin finally looks at me. He gives a smile I can't really see through his beard.

I can't stand it. "So what now?" I ask, because I really want to know what his next move will be.

He ignores my question. "Ah, I almost forgot. That tire mark down on the road. If you take a good look at it, you can tell that the driver turned the wheel at the end like he was pulling into the driveway. But that don't make no sense. Why would the person who set the fire pull into the driveway and not burn rubber all the way to the Georgia line?"

"Couldn't tell you."

"Hhmm." Chief nods like he's thinking. "William, I said earlier that we'd have a lesson today. But the lesson ain't for you. It's for me. I need you to teach me."

"Sir, about the only thing I could teach you is how to sweep a floor or stock shelves." I try to make a joke and laugh through the teeth that have sunk into my stomach.

"That's where you're wrong, William." He turns his whole body square in front of me. His face changes, like a cloud just stopped over his head. "You can teach me why somebody would do this—set fire to a nice family's house, nearly get some homeless man killed, and a pretty young girl and a bunch of kids. I got to know, so why don't you just go ahead and tell me."

I don't say a word.

"I know it was you. I just don't know why. The police

are going to want to know that part, so you might as well practice with me."

"Sir, no. It wasn't me. I would never."

Chief Griffin shakes his head. "You know, I've heard your daddy preach about a thousand sermons it seems like. And there's one he does every year at Easter. It's about Peter denying Jesus three times. Now, Peter swore like everything that he wouldn't do that. But Jesus knew Peter was scared. Like you're scared. But denying don't change the truth. Don't be Peter."

I think about my answer.

"But Chief, denying is what I do best. I deny death when he walks through the door."

"That might be so. But it really don't count when you invite him to the party."

I just stare back at him.

"Get back in the truck, William." He scratches his head. "I should drive you straight to the police station, but I can't do that. Not yet, anyway." He drops his head like I've seen my daddy do when I've done something to disappoint him. "You sure didn't turn out like I expected."

"No one ever does."

THIRTY-THREE

There are some cups we got to drink from whether we want to or not. Sometimes they're the only ones at the table. Kind of like the night before Jesus was crucified. He got down on his knees and prayed that if it was His will, for that particular cup to pass from him. But when it came time, he just didn't drink, he gulped it down in mouthfuls. Well, it's pretty obvious the glass is full—for me and my family.

Samantha does just like I asked and brings Steven over for dinner tonight. I think maybe she got her feelings a little hurt because I didn't invite her too, but she's got her own fires to put out.

I didn't really give anybody a choice in the matter. From

calling Mr. Whitehead at the D&G and telling him I wasn't coming in after school, to Steven showing up at the front door, I pretty much gave everybody their orders. Thank the good Lord each one decided a meal wasn't worth fighting about. Daddy of course grumbled a little but gave in, maybe because he thinks he can save Steven. Truth be told, I'm hoping they didn't resist because they want this supper as bad as I do. They just don't have the gumption or the words to say it.

"It's safe to come in?" Steven asks when I open the door.

"Yeah, no problems at all."

He comes in and looks from side to side like he's walking into the lion's den. I throw my arm around his shoulder. "Really, man, it's fine."

Steven doesn't reply. He looks into the kitchen to see Mom putting ice in the glasses and grabbing napkins like this is the most normal evening ever. Daddy, of course, waits in his office to be called to the table.

Steven takes a deep breath and nods. "Okay." He turns around, opens the door, and waves at Samantha, who's waiting with her car running. When he shuts the door, he says, "Just wanted to make sure I wasn't walking into a catastrophe."

Mom gets the glasses and napkins on the table and comes over to hug Steven's neck. "I've missed you, son," she says in a low voice, like it's a secret. "Go, go sit down." She immediately calls for Daddy to come to the table.

Daddy speaks the first words at the table. "Let us bow

our heads." But he doesn't hold out his hands for us to join. I know it breaks Steven's heart.

We drop our heads. Daddy doesn't speed through the blessing like normal, and he even adds, "And Lord, please help us see the error of our ways" at the end. But I know he doesn't really mean "us."

We begin to eat in a silence that nearly pierces the skin. This is the last meal that will be served at this table. I'm the only one who knows this, of course, which makes it easier to break the rules for acceptable conversation.

"So, when are the two of you going to forgive each other?"

Steven and Daddy look up at me, and then at each other.

"It's not me he should be seeking forgiveness from." Daddy speaks in a flat, even tone that is, at least, void of anger.

"I already have," Steven says to me.

I let everyone continue to eat, waiting to see if anyone has anything else to say. But they don't want to talk. I think they just want to survive this meal and walk away, ignoring the chasm that is this house. No amount of furniture and food and dishes and televisions could come close to filling it. I just keeping looking at Mom, Daddy, Steven, giving anything for them to look up and see each other.

"Hey," I say, loud enough to startle them. *Bang*, I hit the table. "What the hell is wrong with ya'll?"

Samantha was right. Faces tell the truth. They're lost.

I stare at each of them. Finally, Mom says, "Not at the table, William."

"I figure this is as good a place as any, while we're all here facing each other."

"Please," Mom says.

"Listen to your mother," Daddy says in that tone he used when I was a kid. It says, "If you don't do what your mother wants, you'll have to deal with me."

But I'm not a kid anymore, and I'd like to deal with him.

"I'm just confused is all." I turn toward Daddy. "It seems easier for you to have compassion and understanding for folks you hardly know than your own blood."

Daddy sets his knife and fork down on the table. "Son, be careful where you're pointing fingers."

"I don't have to be, Daddy. I'm pointing fingers at all of us."

Mom and Steven are frozen in their seats like wax figures in a museum. *Everyone, here we have dinner time with a typical Southern family.*

"All the time you told me and Steven, 'Remember who you are.' Do *you* remember who we are? Here, let me introduce everybody."

I wipe my hands on my napkin and set it next to my plate. I look over at Daddy and expect to see steam coming off the top of his head to match his pile of mashed potatoes. "This is Steven, your son. He's gay. He's a terrific human being, better than most actually. You should be proud of him. Over here, this is Connie, your wife.

Unfortunately, Connie hasn't been happy for a long time. So she's been seeking happiness at the bottom of a bottle, but her family won't do anything about it, especially her loving and forgiving husband."

That one sucks the air right out of the room. Daddy slams his hand down on the table to shut me up. But I don't stop.

"And over here, we have Pastor Tucker. Steven, Connie, I'd like for you take notice of the man of the house. Please congratulate him on raising a family he can't stand to acknowledge."

That one makes his chair fly backwards. "Let me tell you something..."

"And me. Hey Daddy, I'm William. Some people call me Wee Wee. Your other son. I'm a firefighter. I save lives. Can you see us?"

Daddy's face twists and contorts, making visible the tornado underneath.

"What do you see?" I ask. "WHAT DO YOU SEE?"

"Right now, I see a boy who has forgotten his place." He pushes me and we stare each other down. We're breathing hard, neither one willing to look away for a second.

"Actually, my place couldn't be more clear."

I don't know how many seconds go by before Mom says, "Please, please, can you just sit back down? Can we finish eating?"

I almost laugh. That's what seems to matter right now— the meal, our manners, anything but the truth.

Daddy sits down and gathers himself as quickly as he exploded.

But I don't sit. "Excuse me."

I turn to go to the bathroom, but stop. I have to say one more thing.

"I'm sorry. But I had to."

Nobody says a word.

In the bathroom, I open the cabinet under the sink. One of the things me and Steven learned early on about our mom, and apparently lots of other alcoholics, is she loves to hide bottles all over the house. We never could play a game of hide-and-go-seek without stumbling across a handful of half-empty bottles. The hiding places changed, but the bathroom was consistent as the sun. It's the only room in the house where a person can shut and lock the door and nobody wonders why.

From behind two stacks of towels, I pull out a bottle of gin that's three-quarters full. I know at the last supper there was wine, but this will have to do. Back in the hallway, I stop and listen. Not a sound comes from the kitchen, which means they're all just sitting there, probably trying to handle that much reality all at once.

I step over into my bedroom. I was a good boy today and made up the bed. I kind of chuckle because one of the phrases Daddy used, to help teach Steven and me to face the consequences of our actions, was "Well, you've made your bed, now you got to lie in it." That's probably why I never made my bed. But today is different. It's perfect now, ready and waiting.

I shut the door, lock it, and then unscrew the top off the bottle of gin. Sitting in the middle of the bed, I empty the bottle on the carpet around the bed. Pull some matches out of my pocket.

One last fire. Another baptism. For me, my family. Cleansed of the past.

I strike the match and smile. The flame is a good friend. But what really matters comes after the burn.

About the Author

A native Mississippian, Heath Gibson discovered the joy of children's literature as an adult. Since falling in love with the genre, he has used the unique landscape, people, and voices of the South to fuel his writing. He attributes his storytelling to his childhood dinner table, where jokes and conversations were more important than the fried chicken and mashed potatoes. He currently lives outside Atlanta, Georgia, and tries to teach his students how to make their own discoveries.

Gibson's first novel, *Gigged*, was published in 2010. Visit the author online at www.heathgibson.com.